Romantic Getaways
Escape to Paradise!

This Valentine's Day, escape to four of the world's most romantic destinations with these sparkling books from Harlequin Romance!

From the awe-inspiring desert to vibrant Barcelona, from the stunning coral reefs of Australia to heart-stoppingly romantic Venice, get swept away by these wonderful romances!

The Sheikh's Convenient Princess
by Liz Fielding

The Unforgettable Spanish Tycoon
by Christy McKellen

The Billionaire of Coral Bay
by Nikki Logan

Her First-Date Honeymoon
by Katrina Cudmore

Dear Reader,

Welcome to Venice, the floating city of romance.

One of my all-time favorite movies is *Summertime* (1955) directed by David Lean. The beauty and mystique of Venice plays a vital role in this wonderfully romantic movie, so I was thrilled when my editor, the brilliant Laura McCallen, asked if I would like to base a book in this breathtaking city.

In *Summertime* Katharine Hepburn plays Jane Hudson, a lonely American secretary who travels to Venice full of dreams for romance. In contrast, my heroine, runaway bride Emma Fox, travels to Venice resolute that she will never dare to dream again. But spending a whirlwind week in the company of charismatic tycoon Matteo Vieri during *Carnevale di Venezia* takes Emma to the edge of breaking her resolution. Will she dare to dream again? And will Matteo be able to confront his own demons to reveal his true self behind the mask he wears?

As I wrote this book I became totally captivated by the love story that unfurled between Emma and Matteo; and I hope you do, too, as you read their story.

My warmest wishes until we speak again.

Katrina

Her First-Date Honeymoon

—

Katrina Cudmore

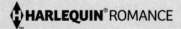

Recycling programs
for this product may
not exist in your area.

ISBN-13: 978-0-373-74423-7

Her First-Date Honeymoon

First North American Publication 2017

Copyright © 2017 by Katrina Cudmore

HARLEQUIN®

www.Harlequin.com

Printed in U.S.A.

A city-loving book addict, peony obsessive **Katrina Cudmore** lives in Cork, Ireland, with her husband, four active children and a very daft dog. A psychology graduate with an MSc in human resources, Katrina spent many years working in multinational companies and can't believe she is lucky enough now to have a job that involves daydreaming about love and handsome men! You can visit Katrina at katrinacudmore.com.

Books by Katrina Cudmore

Harlequin Romance

Swept into the Rich Man's World
The Best Man's Guarded Heart

Visit the Author Profile page at Harlequin.com.

For Ben

See, the middle child isn't always forgotten!

Love, Mum

CHAPTER ONE

'I ADMIRE YOUR TENACITY, *cara*, but I meant it when I said no.'

Matteo Vieri lay down and spread his body behind the woman already warming his bed. His hand curled around her slim waist. The only light in the room came from the corridor, and in the dark shadows, with her head tucked low into the pillow, he struggled to see her in detail. But beneath his fingers he felt her body edge towards him.

Irritation bit into his stomach and refused to let go, but he forced his voice to remain a low playful tease. 'The last woman who crept into my bed wasn't seen for days. Leave now, or I swear you won't see daylight for a very long time.'

He wanted nothing but to sleep. Alone.

Earlier, when she had phoned him while he was en route to Venice, she had told him she was leaving tomorrow for her home city of New York, but she had promised him a night to remember. They had dated intermittently in the past, when their paths had crossed. It had been fun. But recently he had realised that beneath her cool sass lay fantasies of a future together, so he had good-humouredly turned down her offer. Again. But she obviously hadn't listened and now she lay in his bed.

He stifled a curse.

It was past midnight. His bones ached for a shower and the oblivion of sleep.

'*Cara*, it's time for you to leave.'

Beneath the silk of her nightgown her ribcage jerked.

His hand stilled.

Something was wrong. Her scent was wrong. The dip of her waist was wrong. The endless curls in her hair, brushing his hand, making him itch with the desire to thread it through his fingers and pull her towards him, were wrong.

His breathing, his heart, his thoughts went on hold. The red traffic lights of confusion waited to switch to the green of clarity.

Her head inched upwards until wide eyes met his: perplexed, scared, startled.

His own disbelief left him speechless.

Caspita! Who was this stranger lying in his bed?

And then he wanted to laugh. Could this week get any worse?

His starved lungs sucked in air. He could barely make out her features, but still a lick of attraction barrelled through him. Her scent—the clean low notes of rose—the enticing warmth of her body, the mass of hair tumbling on the bed sheets made him want to draw her into him. To take solace in her softness, her femininity, from the craziness of his life.

Her mouth opened. And closed. She swallowed a cartoon gulp. Her mouth opened again. Her lips were full, the hint of a deep cupid's bow on the upper lip. A dangerous beauty.

Her body stiffened beside him. Seconds passed. Two strangers. In the most intimate of settings.

A tiny sound of disbelief hiccupped from her throat.

Then, in a shower of rising and falling sheets and blankets, she flung off the bedclothes and darted towards the door.

In one smooth movement he followed her and yanked her back.

Long narrow bones crashed into him, along with a tumble of hair, a scent that left him wanting more.

'Who are you? What do you want?'

Her voice was a husky rasp, heavily accented, sexy, English. A voice he had definitely never heard before.

Attraction kicked again. Strong enough to knock him out of his stupor. His earlier frustration lit up inside him. Bright and fierce.

He pulled her towards the wall and flicked on the bedroom chandelier. She winced, but then hazel eyes settled on his, anger mixing with shock.

She attempted to jerk away but he gripped her slim arm tighter.

A flare of defiance grew in her eyes. 'If you don't let me go I'm going to scream until the entire neighbourhood, all of Venice, is awake.'

A growl of fury leapt from his throat. 'Scream away. My neighbours are used to hearing me entertain.'

A blush erupted on her cheeks. She dipped her head.

Satisfaction twitched on his lips. He lowered his mouth towards her ear. 'Now, tell me, do you make a habit of breaking into homes? Sleeping in strangers' beds?'

Emma Fox knew she should be scared. But instead an anger, a rebellion, surged in her. She was *not* going to be pushed around again. Her heart might be doing a full drama queen routine in her chest, but the pit of her stomach was shouting, *Enough!* Enough of false accusations. Enough of people telling her what to do. Enough of the mess that was her life.

She grabbed the hand clinging to her upper arm and tried to prise his fingers away. 'What on earth are you talking about? I haven't broken in. I was invited to stay here by the *palazzo*'s owner.'

Her captor took a step back to stare down at her, but his grip grew tighter. For the first time she saw his face. Her heart went silent. Why couldn't he be on the wrong side of handsome? A few blemishes here and there, a little cross-eyed, perhaps. Instead she faced a gulp-inducing, knee-knocking magnificence that stole all her composure.

His golden-brown eyes flared with the incredulous impatience of a man used to getting his way. 'Signorina, that is impossible. *I* own Ca' Divina. This is *my* property.'

He let go of her arm and moved to the door. He slammed it shut and stood guard in front of the large ancient door, arms crossed.

'Now, tell me the truth before I call the *carabinieri*.'

The *carabinieri*. He couldn't. Her stomach tumbled. She had spent a nightmare morning in police custody only yesterday. She couldn't go through *that* again. The disbelieving looks. Then the impatient pity when they'd realised she was nothing but a patsy in the whole debacle.

Fear tap-danced down her spine and she began to shiver. She was wearing only a barely there nightdress and longed to cover up. To walk away from this fully clothed man, armoured in an impeccable dark navy suit and maroon tie, and from the way his eyes were travelling down her body critically. Something about him triggered a memory of seeing him before—but where? Why did he seem familiar?

She backed towards the bed, away from him, and spoke in a rush of words. 'I'm telling the truth. But how do I know who you are—perhaps *you're* the one who has broken into the *palazzo*.'

He threw her an *are you being serious?* look. 'And I've woken you up to have an argument? Not the usual behaviour of a thief, I would expect.'

'No, but—'

He rocked on his heels and inhaled an exasperated breath. 'In my bedside table you'll find a tray of cufflinks with my monogram—MV.'

She opened the top drawer of the lacquered and gilt carved bedside table with trembling fingers. Beside a number of priceless-looking Rolex watches sat a platoon of silver, gold and platinum cufflinks, all bearing the letters MV.

A sinking feeling moved through her body, draining her of all energy. 'I don't understand…I was in a café earlier today and a lady… Signora…'

Her mind became a black hole of forgetfulness. Across from her, her prison guard scowled in disbelief. Flustered, she tried to zone him out. She had to concentrate. What had her saviour's name been?

'Her name was Signora... Signora Ve... Vieri... Yes, that was it—Signora Vieri.'

He unfurled his arms and walked towards her across the antique Oriental rug covering the *terrazzo* floor. A treasure perhaps imported when the Venetian Republic had been the exploration and commercial powerhouse of Europe centuries ago.

His mouth was a thin line of frustration, his already narrow lips tight and unyielding. 'What did this Signora Vieri look like?'

His words were spoken in a low, dangerous rumble and she became unaccountably hot, with flames of heat burning up her insides at the menace in his words and the way he was now standing over her, staring down, as if ready to murder the nearest person.

Her vow to toughen up, to refuse to kowtow to anyone ever again was going to be tested sooner than she had anticipated. She squared her shoulders and looked him right in the eye. Which was a bad idea, because immediately she lost herself in those almond-shaped golden-brown eyes and forgot what she was going to say.

The anger in his eyes turned for the briefest moment into a flare of appreciation. Her heart swooped up her throat like a songbird.

But then the appreciation flicked to exasperation. 'I don't have all night.'

Toughen up. That was her mission in life now. She had to remember that. She clenched her fists and tossed her head back, ready for battle. 'I have no idea what's going on here but, despite what you obviously think, I have not been involved in anything untoward. Signora Vieri offered me a place to stay. I accepted her offer in good faith.'

He loomed over her, tension bouncing off his huge, formidable body. 'Tell me what she looked like...or is this just a convenient story? Perhaps you'll be more co-operative for the *carabinieri*.'

Alarm shot down through her and exited at her toes, leaving a numb, tingling sensation behind. She began to babble. 'She's in her early fifties...animated, kind, concerned...full of energy. Brown bobbed hair. She has the cutest little dog called Elmo.'

He exhaled another loud breath and walked away.

She spun around to find him standing before the bedroom's marble fireplace. The huge gilt mirror on the mantel reflected his powerful tense shoulders, the glossy thickness of his brown hair.

'My grandmother.'

'*Your grandmother!* She mentioned that her grandson sometimes stays here...I was picturing a toddler. Not a grown man.'

For a few long seconds he stopped and glared

at her, leaving her in no doubt that she had said something wrong. What, she had no idea, but the temperature in the room had dropped at least ten degrees.

'*Nonnina* is sixty-seven. And she has a soft spot for waifs and strays. Although this is the first time she has actually brought home a human one.'

'I'm not a waif or a stray!'

'Then what are you doing in my bed?'

Memories of his hand burning through the material of her nightdress, of the shaming stream of pleasure that had flowed through her dreams until she had woken fully taunted her, causing her confusion to intensify.

'Who did you think was in your bed when you climbed in beside me?'

Her question earned her a tight-lipped scowl. 'A friend.'

Unease swept over her at the prospect of that huge, frankly scary-looking lion's head brass knocker on the front door sounding at any moment, and having to explain her presence to another person tonight.

'Are you still expecting her?'

His eyes swept over her lazily. 'No.'

Every inch of her skin tingled. For a moment she gazed longingly towards her suitcase, propped open beside an ornately carved walnut dressing table. She hadn't had the energy to unpack earlier, but had fallen into bed after a much needed shower instead.

She moved towards the suitcase, aware he was following her every move. She grabbed the first jumper from the messy jumble spilling from it and pulled on the thick-knit polo neck. A shiver of comfort and relief ran down her spine; she no longer felt so susceptible to his dangerous gaze.

He moved back across the room towards the door. 'I need to speak to my grandmother.'

'She isn't here.'

He pulled up short. 'What do you mean, she isn't here?'

'She said she had to return home to Puglia. That there was an emergency.'

He shook his head in disgust and twisted away. He rolled his shoulders and then his spine in a quick, impatient movement, the fine wool of his suit jacket rippling in a fluid motion. He moved with the ease of the super-rich. Even his hair—a perfect one-inch length, tapering down in a perfect straight line to hug the tanned strength of his neck—looked as though it had been cut with diamond-encrusted scissors by a barber to the nobility of Europe.

This room—this *palazzo*, this stunning city La Serenissima—all so grand and overwhelming, proud and mysterious, suited him. Whereas *she* felt like an alien amongst the wealth and elegance.

Wealth. Elegance. A grandmother with the surname of Vieri...

Her brain buzzed with the white noise of astonishment while her heart jumped to a *thumpety-thumpety-thump* beat. No wonder he looked familiar.

'You're Matteo Vieri, aren't you?'

The owner of one of the world's largest luxury goods conglomerates.

He unbuttoned his suit jacket and popped a hand into his trouser pocket. 'So you know who I am?' His casual stance belied the sharp tone of his response.

Did he think she had engineered her stay here because of who he was? Engineered being in his bed for his arrival? Did he think she had designs on him romantically? That possibility, if it hadn't been so tragic, would have been laughable.

'I used to work at St Paul's Fashion College in London. One of your companies—VMV—sponsors its graduation show.'

'*Used* to work?'

'I left last week to move to Sydney.'

Well, that had been the plan anyway. Until it had all fallen apart. When was life going to start co-operating with her, instead of throwing her endless grenades of disastrous calamity?

Yet more uncomfortable heat threaded along her veins. She had slept in *Matteo Vieri's* bed.

He was one of Europe's most eligible bachelors. She needed to clarify how all this had happened.

'Your grandmother told me I was welcome to use any room I wanted. I didn't realise this room was yours.' She paused and gestured around the room to the walnut four-poster bed, the pale green silk sofa—all so beautiful, but without a trace of him. 'None of your belongings are on display, no clothes...I had no idea it might be someone's bedroom.'

'When this *palazzo* was built in the fifteenth century not much thought was given to adjoining dressing rooms...my clothes are further down the hallway.' He spoke like a bored tour guide, tired of the same inane tourist questions.

'But your bathroom is full of...' She trailed off, not sure how to say it. It was full of delicious but most definitely girly shampoos and conditioners, bath and shower gels, lavish body lotions...

He gave her a *don't push it* frown. 'I do own those companies.' His lips moved for a nanosecond upwards into the smile of a man remembering good times. 'Those products are there for my dates to use.'

She tugged at the collar of her jumper, feeling way too hot. The image of a naked Matteo Vieri applying one of those shower gels was sending her pulse into the stratosphere.

She went to her suitcase and squashed the lid

down, fighting the giddiness rampaging through her limbs, praying it would zip up without its usual fight.

'I'll move to another room.'

He stood over her, casting a dark shadow over her where she crouched. 'I'm afraid that's not an option. You'll have to leave.'

She sprang up, her struggle with the suitcase forgotten. 'But I have nowhere to go! I spent all of today searching for a hotel, but with it being Carnival time there are no rooms available. I've tried everywhere within my budget. Meeting your grandmother…her kind offer of a room was like a miracle.'

'I bet it was—an invitation to stay in a *palazzo* on the Grand Canal in Venice!'

Did he *have* to sound so cynical? 'I appreciate this situation is far from ideal, but I have nowhere else to go. I promise I'll stay out of your way.'

He adjusted the cuffs of his shirt beneath his suit jacket with a stiff, annoyed movement. His cufflinks flashed beneath the light of the crystal chandelier. 'I apologise for my grandmother's behaviour. She shouldn't have given you a room without my authorisation. I have a busy week ahead, with clients from China coming to Venice for Carnival. It does not suit me to have a house guest.'

'Are they staying here?'

'No, but—'

'Honestly—I've tried every hotel in Venice.'

He glared at her, and for a moment she was transported back to her *pointe* classes as an eleven-year-old, when she used to shake with fear about getting on the wrong side of the volatile ballet master.

'Why are you in Venice, Signorina…?' His voice trailed off and he waited for her to speak.

'Fox. Emma Fox. I'm here because…' A lump the size of the top tier of her wedding cake formed in her throat. She gritted her teeth against the tears blurring her vision. 'I was supposed to be here on my honeymoon.'

His stomach did a nosedive. *Dio!* She was about to cry.

Something about the way she was fighting her tears reminded him of his childhood, watching his mother battle her tears. Unable to do anything to stop them. To make life okay for her. Not sure why she was crying in the first place when he was a small boy other than having a vague understanding that she was waiting for his father to come back. The father he'd never known.

And then in later years, when she had accepted that his father was never going to return, her tears had been shed over yet another failed relationship. But he hadn't even tried to comfort her in those years. His own pain had been too great—pain for all the men who had walked out of his life without a fight, father figures, many of whom he had hero-worshipped.

People let you down. It was a lesson he had learned early in life. Along with coming to the realisation that he could only ever rely on himself. Not trust in the empty promises of others.

A loud sniffle brought him back to his present problem. To her lowered head he said, 'On your honeymoon?'

She emitted a cry and bolted for his bathroom.

This time his grandmother had gone too far. To the extent that he was tempted to follow her down to Puglia and give her a piece of his mind, this time not falling for her apologies and pledges to behave. Nor, for that matter, being diverted by plates of her legendary *purcedduzzi*—fried gnocchi with honey.

He understood her compulsion to help the poor and homeless—but to invite a stranger into his *home*!

He knocked at the bathroom door. 'Are you okay?'

'Yes…sorry. I'll be out in a few minutes.'

Her voice went from alto to soprano, and several notes in between. A muffled sob followed. He winced and rubbed at his face with both hands.

He leaned in against the door. 'We both need

a drink. Join me downstairs in the lounge when you're ready.'

He hurried down the stairs. Memories chased him. Those nights when he was seven…eight years old, when he would crawl into his mother's bed, hoping he could stop her tears.

In the lounge, he threw open the doors onto the terrace. Venice was blanketed in a light misty fog. Sounds were muffled. He saw the intermittent lights of a launch moving on the water, its engine barely audible. Technically it was spring, but tonight winter still shrouded the city, and the cold, damp air intensified its mysterious beauty.

He spent most of his year travelling between his headquarters in Milan and his offices in New York, London and Paris. Always moving. Never belonging. The nomadic lifestyle of his childhood had followed him into adulthood. He had hated it as a child. Now it suited him. It meant that he could keep a distance from others. Even acquaintances and those he considered friends would never have the opportunity to hurt him, to walk away. *He* was the one in control instead. It was *he* who could choose to walk away now.

Venice was his one true escape. It was why he had no regular staff here in Ca' Divina. He liked the calm, the peace of the building, without sound, without people awaiting his instructions. Here was the one place he could be alone, away from the intensity of his normal routine. Away from the constant expectations and responsibilities of his businesses, his family.

But tonight the calm serenity of both Venice and Ca' Divina were doing little to calm his boiling irritation. The maverick, eccentric, brilliant chief designer for his fashion house Ettore had thrown a hissy fit—no doubt fuelled by alcohol—whilst being interviewed by a Chinese news team last night. He had not only insulted the reporter but also implied that the exclusive department store chain that sold his designs in China was not worthy of doing so.

The exclusive department store chain Matteo was delicately negotiating with over contracts for the extensive expansion of product placement for *all* his brands.

The company quite rightly had not taken kindly to the designer's words, and had seen it as a huge public insult to their honour. This loss of face—known as *mianzi* in China—might have damaged their relationship beyond repair.

The chain's president and his team were arriving in Venice tomorrow evening. He had a lot of apologising to do and reassurances to make to ensure they understood how much he valued and respected them as a partner. It was vital the trip went well. Or else several of his lines would be in serious financial trouble.

He twisted around to the sound of footsteps on the *terrazzo* flooring. The last thing he needed was to have to deal with a stranger's problems.

She reminded him of a Federico Zandomeneghi portrait in Ca' Pesaro, the International Gallery of Modern Art located further along the banks of the Grand Canal. Delicate, elegant features, a cupid's bow mouth, a perfect nose, porcelain skin, long thick brown curls almost to her waist, tucked behind her ears.

Below the cream polo-neck jumper she was now wearing a pair of skinny jeans and tan ankle boots. She'd tugged the neck of the jumper up until it reached her ears. The tears were gone, but despite the resolute set of her mouth she looked worn out.

Almost as worn out as *he* felt.

'What can I get you to drink?'

'A whisky, please.'

He poured her whisky and a brandy for himself into tumblers, trying to ignore how physically aware he was of her. Of her refined accent, her words clipped but softly spoken. Of her long limbs. Of the outline of the tantalising body her nightdress had done little to conceal earlier. Of her utter beauty.

He brought their drinks over to the sofas at the centre of the room and placed one on either side of the coffee table in between them. He sat with his back to the canal.

She perched on the side of the sofa and stared out through the terrace windows with an unseeing gaze, the hands on her lap curled like weapons ready to strike out. Eventually her eyes landed on his, and the sudden flare of vulnerability in them delivered a sucker punch to his gut.

Despite every fibre of his being telling him not to—she might start crying again—he found himself asking, 'Do you want to talk about it?'

She took a sip of her whisky. Depositing the glass back on the table, she reached down to her left ankle and gave it a quick squeeze. Sitting up, she inhaled deeply, her chest rising and falling. A flash of heat coloured her cheeks. The result of the whisky or something else?

'Not particularly.' Her clipped tone was accompanied by a haughty rise of her chin.

'In that case I'll go and make some phone calls to arrange a hotel room for you.'

He was at the door before she spoke.

'My fiancé…I mean my *ex*-fiancé…was arrested early yesterday morning—at four o'clock, to be precise—for embezzlement.'

She tugged at the neck of her jumper. He returned to his seat and she darted a quick glance in his direction. Pride in battle with pain.

'He stole funds from the company he worked

for; and also persuaded his family and friends to invest in a property scheme with him. There was no scheme. Instead he used the money to play the stock exchange. He lost it all.'

'And you knew nothing about it?'

She stared at him aghast. 'No!' Then she winced, and the heat in her cheeks noticeably paled. 'Although the police wouldn't believe me at first...' She glanced away. 'I was arrested.'

'Arrested?'

She reached for her glass but stopped halfway and instead edged further back into the sofa. 'Yes, arrested. On what was supposed to be my wedding day.' She gave a disbelieving laugh. 'I was let go eventually, when they realised I was his victim rather than his partner in crime.'

Her eyes challenged his; she must be seeing the doubt in his expression.

'By all means call Camden Police Station in London, if you don't believe me; they will verify my story. I have the number of the investigating officer.'

His instinct told him she was telling the truth, but he wasn't going to admit that. 'It's of no consequence to me.'

That earned him a hurt glance. Remorse prickled along his skin. But why was he feeling guilty? None of this was his doing. What on earth was she doing in Venice anyway?

'Do you think it was wise, coming to Venice? Without a hotel booking? Wouldn't you be better off at home?'

She crossed her legs with an exasperated frown that told him he wasn't getting this. 'I *did* have a hotel booking. Or so my ex told me. But he never transferred the funds so the booking fell through. He also cleared out our joint bank account. Anyway, I don't *have* a home. Or a job. I moved out of my apartment and resigned from the college because my ex was being transferred to Sydney with his work and I was joining him.'

'And your family?'

A flicker of pain crossed her face. But then she sat upright and eyed him coolly. 'I don't have one.'

Despite all the hurts and frustrations of the past, and the fact that he had far from perfect relationships with his emotional and unpredictable mother and grandmother, he could never imagine life without them. What must it be like to have no family? Had she no friends who could take their place?

'Your friends…?'

With her legs crossed, she rotated her left ankle in the air. Agitated. Upset.

'I appreciate your concern, but I'm not going back to London. I have no home to go to. I can't go back…I can't face everyone. I need some time away. After I was released from police custody I

checked out of the hotel we'd been staying in…'
She paused and bit her lip, drank some whisky,
grimaced. 'I ran away.'

'You're a runaway bride?'

Her generous full mouth twisted unhappily. She
refused to meet his eye.

'I'm not putting my friends out by sleeping on
their sofas. My closest friend Rachel has just had
a baby; the last thing she needs right now is a
lodger. This is my mess—it's up to me to sort it
out. My ex might have stolen everything from me,
but he isn't going to stop me from living my life.
I've always wanted to see Venice during Carnival. And I fully intend doing so.'

Her mouth gave a little wobble.

'We had organised our wedding for this week
so that it coincided with Carnival.'

She was putting up one hell of a fight to keep
her tears at bay. He felt completely out of his comfort zone.

'I'll pay for your hotel room by way of compen-
sation for any inconvenience my grandmother's
actions may have caused.'

'I don't want your money.'

Old memories churned in his stomach at her
resolve. He knew only too well that it masked
vulnerability.

He remembered throwing guilt money from
Stefano, one of his mother's boyfriends, who had

just shoved it into his hands, off the balcony of Stefano's apartment. He had got momentary satisfaction seeing Stefano's shame. It had been short-lived, though, when he and his mother had been forced to sleep in a homeless hostel that night.

He had stayed awake all night, unable to sleep, vowing he would never be in that position again. Vowing to drag his mother out of poverty and to protect her. Even if her behaviour *had* led them to sharing a room with eight strangers. He would be a success. Which meant he would no longer be held hostage by poverty, by the lack of choices, the motives of other people.

It was an ambition he was still chasing. He still needed to leave behind the spectre of hunger, the fear of not being in control, still needed to prove himself, still needed to make sure he protected his family...and now the tens of thousands who worked for him.

He looked at his watch and then back at her. She was blinking rapidly. Unexpected emotion gripped his throat. He forced it away with a deep swallow. 'It's late. We can talk about this in the morning.'

'I can stay?'

The relief in her face hit him like a punch. This woman needed compassion and care. His grandmother should be here, finishing the task she'd started. Not dumping it on *him*. He was too busy.

In truth, he didn't know how to help her. He didn't get tangled up in this type of situation. He kept others at arm's length. No one got close. Even his mother and grandmother. And that was not going to change.

'You can stay for tonight. Tomorrow I will organise alternative accommodation for you.'

Half an hour later Emma lay on cool sheets in the bed of another bedroom, her mind on fire, wondering if the past few hours had actually happened.

A knock sounded on the door. She sat up and stared at the door dubiously.

'Emma—it's Matteo.'

Her heart flipped in full operatic diva mode. Did he *have* to speak in a voice that sounded as if he was caressing her? And what did he *want*? Had he changed his mind about her staying?

She cautiously opened the door and drank in the sight of Matteo, freshly showered, his thick brown hair damp, wearing nothing but pyjama bottoms. The golden expanse of his hard sculptured torso instantly left her tongue-tied. And guilty. And cross. She should be on honeymoon right now. Not staring at a stranger's body, trying to keep lustful thoughts at bay.

She folded her arms. 'Can I help you?'

Her ice-cool tone did little to melt the amusement in his eyes.

An eyebrow—a beautiful, thick eyebrow—rose. Without a word he raised his hand and held out a toy polar bear, barely the size of his palm, grey and threadbare.

'Snowy!' She grabbed the bear and held it to her chest.

'I found it under my pillow.'

'I forgot about him…thank you.'

His head tilted to the side and for a tiny moment he looked at her with almost affection, but then he looked back at Snowy with an exasperated shake of his head. Probably questioning the wisdom of allowing a grown woman who slept with a diseased-looking toy polar bear to stay in his home.

He turned away.

She should close the door, to signal that his appearance was of little consequence, but instead she watched him walk back to his room—and almost swooned when he ran his hand through his hair, the movement of the powerful muscles in his back taunting her pledge to give men a wide berth.

He swung back to her. 'I'm sorry about your wedding.'

A thick wedge of gratitude landed in her chest. She wanted to say thank you, but her throat was as tight as a twisted rag.

He nodded at her thank-you smile.

Her heart beat slow and hard in her chest.

They stood in silence for far too long.

He seemed as unable to turn away as she was.

Eventually he broke the tension and spoke in a low, rolling tone, *'Buonanotte.'*

Back inside the room, she climbed into bed and tucked Snowy against her. She was fully aware, of course, that the first thing she should do in her bid to toughen up was to banish Snowy from her bed. But when she had been a child, alone and petrified at boarding school, he had brought her comfort. And, rather sadly, over fifteen years on she needed him more than ever before.

So much for Operation Toughen Up. An hour in the company of Matteo Vieri and all her vows and pledges to be resilient and single-minded had melted into a puddle of embarrassing tears and ill-advised attraction.

But tomorrow was going to be different.

It *had* to be.

CHAPTER TWO

THE FOLLOWING DAY, mid-morning sunshine poured into Matteo's office. He stood up from his desk and stretched his back, grimacing at the tightness at the bottom of his spine.

They said bad things came in threes. Well, he had just reached his quota. First, his exasperating but gifted designer had publicly insulted his most valued clients. Then his grandmother had invited a stranger into his home. And now his event co-ordinator for the Chinese clients' trip had gone into early labour.

His designer was already in rehab.

He would have to put in extra hours to ensure the China trip ran perfectly...which meant even less sleep than usual.

And as for Signorina Fox... Well, he had news for her.

He walked down the corridor of the *palazzo*'s first floor, the *piano nobile*, his heels echoing on the heritage *terrazzo* flooring. He hadn't seen or heard from Signorina Fox all morning. He had a sneaking suspicion that she was deliberately staying out of his way in the hope that he might let her stay.

The lounge balcony windows were open. Shouts of laughter and passionate calls tumbled into the room from outside. Stepping into the early spring-time sunshine, he came to an abrupt halt.

Crouched over the balcony, her chin resting on her folded arms Emma was focused on the canal, oblivious to the fact that her short skirt had risen up to give him an uninterrupted view of her legs. Legs encased in thick woollen tights that shouldn't look sexy. But her legs were so long, so toned, that for a brief moment the ludi-crous idea of allowing her to stay and act as a distraction from all his worries flitted through his brain.

He coughed noisily.

She popped up and twisted around to look at him. A hand tugged at her red skirt. Over the skirt she was wearing another polo-necked jumper, today in a light-knit navy blue. Her chestnut hair hung over one shoulder in a thick plait.

'I hope you found my note?'

'Thank you—yes…it was a lovely breakfast.'

The exhaustion of last night was gone from beneath her eyes. She gave him a *can we try to act normal?* smile and then gestured to the canal.

'There's the most incredible flotilla sailing up the canal—you must come and see.' Her smile was transformed into a broad beam, matching the excitement in her eyes. She beckoned him over.

He should get back to work. But it seemed churlish to refuse to look. The canal was teeming with boats, and onlookers were crowding the *fondamente*—the canal pathways.

'It's the opening parade of the Carnival,' he explained.

For a few minutes he forgot everything that was wrong in his life as he joined her in watching the parade of gondolas and ceremonial boats sail past. Most of the occupants, in flamboyant seventeenth-and eighteenth-century costume, waved and shouted greetings in response to Emma's enthusiastic waves.

Seeing the contrast between her upbeat mood now and the sobs that had emanated from his bathroom last night twisted his stomach, along with the memory of his grandmother's words this morning. He had called her with the intention of lambasting her, only to be pulled up short when he'd learned that she had gone home because one of the homeless men she helped had been involved in an accident, and that she had helped Emma because she had found her in a desperate state in a café yesterday.

He pushed away the guilt starting to gnaw a hole in his gut. He had enough problems of his own. Anyway, he didn't do cohabitation. He had never shared his home with anyone. And he wasn't about to start with an emotional runaway bride.

Below them, the regatta started to trail off.

'I have found alternative accommodation for you in the Hotel Leopolda.'

Her smile dropped from her face like a stone sinking in water. 'Hotel Leopolda? The five-star hotel close to St Mark's Square?'

'Yes.'

She stared back at the canal, a small grimace pulling on her mouth. 'I can't afford to stay there.'

'I'll take care of it.'

She stepped away from him before meeting his eye. 'I said it last night—I'm not taking your money.'

'I can appreciate how you feel. If it makes you happier, you can repay me some time in the future.'

'No.' Those hazel eyes sucked him in, dumped a whole load of guilt on his soul and spat him back out again.

'I'll make some calls myself—check the internet again. I'll find somewhere suitable,' she said.

This woman was starting to drive him crazy. He had had to use all his influence to secure her a room. He doubted she would find anywhere by herself.

'I want to resolve this now. My event co-ordinator for the Chinese trip has gone into early labour. I'll be tied up with organising all the final details for the visit for the rest of the day.'

She stepped back towards him, her crossed arms dropping to her sides. Concern flooded her eyes. 'I hope she'll be okay. How many weeks pregnant is she?'

He had no idea. It had been a sizeable bump. Once he had even seen a tiny foot kick hard against the extended bump during a meeting. It had been one of the most incredible things he had ever seen.

That image had haunted him for days afterwards. Catching him unawares in meetings, distracting his concentration. Bringing a hollow sensation to his chest, a tightness to his belly, knowing he would never see the first miraculous stirrings of his own child. Knowing he would never be a father. Knowing he would choose the empty feeling that came with that knowledge over the certain pain of letting someone into his life, of risking his heart in a relationship.

'I'm not sure…eight months?'

Did she *have* to look at him so critically? Suddenly he felt he had to defend himself. 'I asked for flowers to be sent to her.'

'I don't think flowers are allowed in hospitals these days. Anyway, I reckon flowers are the last thing on her mind right now.' She threw him another critical stare before adding, 'I hope she and her baby will be okay.'

Why, all of a sudden, was *he* the villain in all of this? 'Of course I do too. My employees' welfare is of great importance to me. It's why they all receive a comprehensive healthcare package.'

'I'm glad to hear it.' Her tone didn't match her words. Her tone implied he was a close relative of *Wall Street*'s Gordon Gekko.

'About your accommodation…'

'How long are your clients here for?'

Hadn't she heard him? This conversation was supposed to be about her leaving. 'Why do you ask?'

'Have you someone to take over from your event planner?'

A tight dart of pain prodded his lower back. He stretched with a quick movement, but it brought little relief. 'No. My event management team are already stretched, co-ordinating the upcoming spring/summer shows. Most of the team are already in New York, getting ready for the shows there.'

She pulled her lips between her teeth as if in thought. When they popped back out they formed an even fuller pout, had turned a more sensual red than usual. Emphasising their cupid's bow shape. She had a beautiful mouth…

A sudden urge to take her in his arms and

taste those lips gripped him. Maybe he was more stressed than he'd realised?

Emma's mind whirled. Could she drum up the courage to suggest *she* take over the event planner's role? Work for Matteo Vieri? Without question it was what every ambitious marketing assistant dreamt of. She should be genuflecting right now in front of this business legend; this marketing genius, instead of deliberately trying to antagonise him. What was *that* about?

A niggling thought told her that not only was she trying in vain to ignore how attracted she was to him—especially when he openly stared at her with interest, as he was doing right now, with particular attention focused on her mouth— but that it would hurt to have another person reject her. Which, rationally, she knew was crazy. They barely knew each other. But even after so many rejections it still hurt when others turned her away.

Working for him would be the kick-start her career needed. Even a week of working with him would open doors for her.

But she was a mess.

She had come to Venice to heal and to get her game plan together. She felt hollow and abused. She was in no position to deliver the best performance of her career.

A mocking voice echoed in her head. *You said you were going to toughen up. Time for action and a lot less talk.*

And having a purpose, being busy, might stop the stream of guilt and sadness that was constantly threatening to break through her defences—defences of shock and numbness, of a determination to tough it out. Being in control, having a structure to her days, was what she needed.

She spoke before she had time to talk herself out of it. '*I'll* do it.'

His gaze moved from her lips to her eyes. Very slowly. So slowly that time seemed to stand still while her cheeks spontaneously combusted.

'*You?*'

Did he *have* to sound so appalled by her proposal?

'In my role at the fashion college I often helped pull events together—from the graduation show to organising the visits of academics and sponsors. Last year I co-ordinated the visit of some members of a faculty from a Chinese fashion college. I'm in need of a place to stay…you need an event co-ordinator.'

'But you're on holiday.'

'My career is more important. I'll be frank: having the Vieri name on my CV will be priceless.'

He seemed to be considering her proposal. For a moment hope danced before her eyes. But then he cut that hope off at the legs with a single de-termined shake of that movie-star-meets-roman-emperor head.

'It's not a good idea.'

'Why?'

'This trip is of critical importance to my com-panies. The delegation is coming to negotiate con-tracts which would see the large-scale expansion of our product placements in China's most presti-gious department stores. Nothing can go wrong.'

For a moment she considered backing down, admitting that she was probably the wrong per-son for the job. But she had to believe in herself.

'You can brief me on it this morning, and then I'll liaise with the travel agents and hotels in-volved. I'll also double-check that all the pro-tocols involved with hosting Chinese guests are followed. If there are any issues I will notify you immediately.'

He leaned one hip against the balcony and folded his arms. 'It's not a nine-to-five position. You would need to attend all the scheduled events with me.'

'That's no problem.'

Those brown eyes darkened. 'We will be work-ing closely together.'

'That's fine.'

Liar! Why is your belly dancing with giddiness if that is the case?

'Please understand I never mix business with pleasure.'

Why was he telling her that? Was her attraction to him so obvious?

'Of course. Exactly my sentiments.' She took a deep swallow and forced herself to ask, 'So, can I have the job?'

'Tell me why I should give it to you.'

This would be so much easier if he wasn't so gorgeous—if he wasn't so self-assured, so ice-cool.

'I will work myself to the bone for you because I have so much to prove. To you—but especially to myself.'

He stared at her as though she was a discount store garment made of polyester. It looked as if she would be packing soon. A heavy sensation sat on her chest—embarrassment, disappointment.

'As I'm stuck, I'll let you take on the position—but any mishaps and you're gone.'

His scowl told her he wasn't joking. Her ankle and heart began to throb in unison.

He came a little closer. Studied her for far too long for her comfort.

'You will need to stay here…'

For a moment he paused, and a heavy boom of attraction detonated between them. She fell into the brown sultry depths of his eyes. An empty ache coiled through her. Heat licked against her skin. She pulled the neck of her jumper down, suddenly overheating.

Matteo stepped back, tugged at his cuffs and cleared his throat. 'I will require frequent briefings from you, so you will need to stay here. I'm hosting a reception in the ballroom on Thursday night, which I will want you to co-ordinate and host alongside me.' He flicked his hand towards the *palazzo*. 'If you come with me to my office I'll brief you on the event schedule and then pass you the files.'

Emma walked alongside him, her enflamed skin welcoming the shade of the *palazzo*. But her mind continued to race, asking her what on earth she had just done.

Could she keep her promise that nothing would go wrong? What if she slipped up and he saw even a glimpse of how attracted she was to him? An attraction that was embarrassingly wrong. Humiliatingly wrong. Shamefully wrong. She had been about to marry another man yesterday. What was the *matter* with her?

They walked side by side into the deeper shadows of the *palazzo*, and she felt guilt and sadness closing over her heart.

Later that afternoon, his phone to his ear, Matteo walked into the temporary office Emma had set up for herself in the *palazzo*'s dining room.

Sheets of paper were scattered across the table. He tidied the paper into a bundle. A long navy silk crêpe de Chine scarf dotted with bright red gerbera daisy flowers was tossed across the back of a chair, the ends touching against the *terrazzo* flooring. A bright exclamation against the dark wood. He folded it quickly and hid it from view by placing it on the seat of the dining chair.

His call continued to ring unanswered.

Where *was* she?

He had told her to be back at the *palazzo* by four so that he could take her to see his stores on Calle Larga XXII Marzo. She needed to be familiar with his companies and their products before her interactions with the clients.

Before lunch they had spent two hours running through the visit's itinerary. Two hours during which he had questioned his judgement in agreeing to her taking over the event co-ordinator role.

With her every exclamation of delight over the events planned, with every accidental touch as they worked through the files, with every movement that caused her jumper to pull on her breasts he had become more and more fixated with watching her.

And throughout the morning she had progressively impressed and surprised him with her attention to detail. Impressed him because she had picked up on some timing problems he hadn't spotted. Surprised him because, tidiness-wise, the woman was a disaster.

Obviously timekeeping wasn't a strength either.

The Chinese delegation were arriving in Venice this evening. He had to be at Hotel Cipriani at eight to greet them on their arrival. Emma had travelled over there, at her suggestion, after lunch to meet with the hotel co-ordinator and the interpreter employed for the duration of the visit.

He hit the call button again.

After yet more infuriating rings, she eventually answered.

He didn't wait for her to speak, '*Dove sei?* Where are you?'

'I'm not sure.' There was a hint of panic to her voice. 'After my meetings in Hotel Cipriani I decided I would visit the restaurant booked for the clients later this week on Giudecca. I found the restaurant and spoke to the owner and the chef. But when I left I must have gone in the wrong direction, because I'm totally lost. I can't find my way back to the *vaporetto* stop.'

Now he really *was* regretting his decision to employ her. 'Can't you ask someone to help you?'

'I have! But each time I follow their directions I end up even more lost down another narrow alleyway.'

Dio! 'Can you see a street name anywhere?'

'Hold on...yes, I see one! Calle Ca Rizzo.'

'Stay there. I'll come and get you.'

'There's no need. I'll—'

He hung up before she had time to start arguing with him. It was already past four.

Emma placed her phone back into her padded jacket's pocket, her already racing heart now acting as if it was taking part in the international finals of the one hundred metre sprint. The day had been going so well until she had gone and got lost in this warren of laneways or, as they were called locally, *calli* that made up Giudecca, an island suburb of Venice.

Her meetings in the opulent surroundings of Hotel Cipriani had gone smoothly, all the little extras she'd requested had been accommodated, and she had then made her way to Ristorante Beccherie, excited at the stunning views across the water to St Mark's Square, the Basilica di San Marco and the Campanile clearly visible under the clear blue sky.

After her meeting at the restaurant she hadn't minded getting lost at first. She had been enchanted by the three-and four-storey medieval redbrick houses on deserted narrow alleyways, by the washing hanging between the houses like bunting, the endless footbridges crossing over the maze of canals. The lack of the sounds of the twenty-first century because of the absence of cars.

But as she'd grown increasingly disorientated, her uneasiness had increased. She'd ended up in dead-end alleyways, silent and beautiful court-yards with no obvious signage.

Matteo was annoyed with her. No—scratch that. He'd sounded ballistic. Would he fire her on her first day?

She walked over to the canal that ran diago-nally to the start of Calle Ca Rizzo and moved down onto the canal steps. The temperature was dropping and the cold stone bit against her skin.

Matteo was like Venice. Utterly beautiful but completely frustrating. All morning she had tried to remain professional, but she had been con-stantly distracted.

Distracted by his deep, potent musky scent when he moved closer to her to point something out in the file sitting between them.

Distracted by the perfect fit of his grey trousers on his narrow hips when he stood.

Distracted by the sight of his large hand lying on the table beside her: golden skin, wide palm, smooth knuckles, long, strong fingers tapering off into pale pink nails, all perfectly clipped into smooth ovals. Several times she had lost her con-centration to those hands, dreaming about them on her skin, removing her clothes...

She had been glad of an excuse to get away

from the *palazzo*, needing some space to pull herself together.

She dropped her head into her hands. What was she *doing*? Why was she having these thoughts? She wasn't interested in men. In any form of relationship. She had a job to do. And falling for the boss was not only out of the question it was beyond stupid. Well, she *hoped* she still had a job to do. Maybe not when he arrived…

Fifteen minutes later she saw him stop on a footbridge further down the canal and stare towards her. His hip-length black wool pea coat was topped with a dark grey woollen hat. The pull of attraction tugged on every cell in her body. His mouth was turned downwards in a *you're in big trouble* scowl.

She jumped up and tried to match his stride in her direction, but her legs were too wobbly so she careened her way along the canal bank, probably looking as if she had recently consumed a considerable amount of Chianti.

When they met her words of apology became lost. His hat hugged his skull, emphasising the intensity of his golden-brown eyes framed by thick black eyelashes, the beauty of his honey-coloured skin, the proud straight nose, the no-nonsense mouth softened by the cleft in his chin.

That gorgeous mouth hardened. 'We are late for our appointments.'

Did that mean he wasn't going to fire her?

Without another word he walked away and she followed alongside him, over countless bridges and through a maze of *calli*. They passed few people, and in the tight confines of the laneways he seemed taller and more powerful than she remembered.

She gave a quick summary of her meetings, updating him on any changes. Hoping his mood might improve. He made no comment but gave an occasional nod. At least he was listening.

Eventually they arrived at the broad reach of Canale della Giudecca and he led her to a sleek, highly polished wooden motor boat moored at a landing stage.

After untying the two mooring ropes he held the stern tight against the wooden stage. He held out his hand to her. 'You need to climb aboard.'

She hesitated for a moment, suddenly wary of touching him. But, with the boat swaying in the choppy waters, she decided she'd risk holding his hand over the chagrin of being crushed against the landing stage.

His hand encased hers, and his powerful strength guided her on board. For a crazy few seconds she was engulfed by the sensation that she would always be safe with him in her life.

With practised ease Matteo pulled the boat

away from the stage and was soon heading across the canal towards St Mark's Square.

'I'm sorry I got lost. I didn't mean to inconvenience you.'

He gave that ubiquitous continental shrug that might mean he accepted her apology with some reservations or was so irritated by her that he couldn't speak.

At first she thought he was going back up the Grand Canal to Ca' Divina, but just west of St Mark's Square he turned right and slowly motored up a smaller canal. The canal was busy with gondolas, the majority of their passengers embracing and kissing couples.

She plucked her phone out of her pocket and pressed some buttons mindlessly. She had thought she wouldn't mind seeing couples together, enjoying this city of romance. Boy, had she been wrong.

A heavy pain constricted her chest.

She was supposed to be here with her husband. Not with a man who was clearly irritated with her. Not with a man who in truth she was more attracted to than she had ever been to her fiancé.

That truth was shaming.

That truth was bewildering.

'As I explained this morning, five of my companies have a presence here on Calle Larga.'

Matteo came to a stop outside the type of store Emma would window shop at when walking along Bond Street in London but would never dare to enter, knowing her monthly salary wouldn't even buy her a set of barely there but, oh, so gorgeous underwear.

He pointed along the bustling street. 'Verde for handbags, Marco for shoes, Osare is the label for our younger urban clients… Gioiello stocks day-wear, and…' Gesturing to the store behind them, he added, 'And VMV for the discerning.'

Was he aware of the constant looks of appreciation he received from passers-by? How within the VMV store a bevy of model-like assistants were flapping their arms in excitement at his imminent entrance?

'I had hoped to take you into each store so that you could familiarise yourself with our product range.' He threw her a reproachful frown. 'But that will not be possible now. We only have time for your fittings.'

With that he turned, and the door of the store was magically opened by a stealthy doorman Emma hadn't seen lurking behind the glass pane.

Matteo gestured for her to enter first.

She took a step closer to him and in a low voice asked, 'What do you mean, "fittings"?'

'You will need dresses and gowns for the various events you will be accompanying me to during the week.'

'I have my own clothes.'

With a raised critical eyebrow he ran his gaze down over her body. Okay, so her black padded jacket and red skirt mightn't be the most glamorous, but she did own some nice clothes.

'I mean I have suitable dresses back at the *palazzo*.'

He stepped closer, his huge body dwarfing hers. His head dipped down and he glared into her eyes. 'I don't have time for this. Let me be clear. You are representing my companies this week. You have to wear clothing from the lines. It's not negotiable. If you don't like it then I'm happy for you to leave.'

Emma gave a quick nod and, with dread exploding in her stomach like fast-rising dough, stepped inside the store and sank into plush carpet. She opened up her padded jacket and yanked at the collar of her jumper. She was burning up. Not only from the heat of the store but from the unfriendly gazes being thrown in her direction by the models.

Matteo walked through the store, pointing out garments which were immediately whisked away to the rear of the store.

'*Bene*. I've selected the gowns which I think will suit you.' He exchanged some rapid words with the woman who had accompanied him in his selection of dresses. 'Andreina will help you try them on.'

Emma smiled warily at the six foot ash blonde diva standing before her. In return she received a cool blue stare. Boy, was she glad she had been waxed to within an inch of her life in preparation for her wedding.

The fitting room was like nothing she had ever seen. A bottle of Prosecco on ice sat on an antique side table, with velvet grey chairs at either side. The floor was tiled in marble, and giant gilt-edged mirrors filled three walls.

She looked at the row of dresses awaiting her. And then at Andreina, who was staring down at her ankle boots, her forehead pinched in obvious disbelief at the water stains on the suede. Yeah, well, maybe Andreina should try walking from Camden Police Station to Highgate in icy slush.

Her stomach lurched. She felt like a gauche fourteen-year-old again, facing her mother's critical stare. Forced to wear only what her mother approved of.

Time for Operation Toughen Up again.

She propelled Andreina by the elbow towards the door. 'I'll call you if I need any help.' She closed the door on a stream of Italian protest, adrenaline pumping.

She approached the dresses warily. She would

get this over and done with as quickly as possible. She stripped off her clothes and grabbed the first dress to hand. Her stomach lurched again. She pulled the silk bodice over her head, felt layer upon layer of fine tulle falling from her waist down to the floor. She twisted her arms around to her back in an attempt to tie the bodice but it was hopeless. She needed help.

She fought against the tears stinging her eyes. She couldn't bear the feel of the material on her skin.

A knock sounded on the door. She ignored it.

'Emma, what are you doing?'

Matteo.

She called out, 'None of them suit. I'll just have to wear my own clothes.'

The door swung open.

'For crying out loud, Matteo, I could have been undressed!'

He crossed the room towards her, his eyes darkening. 'I see near-naked models backstage at fashion shows all the time.'

'Well, I'm *not* a model, am I?'

His mouth pursed, and then he asked with irritation, 'Why are you upset?'

'I'm not.'

He threw her an exasperated look. 'That dress is perfect for you—what do you mean, it doesn't suit? Look in the mirror and see for yourself.'

She turned her back on the mirrors, refusing to look, unable to speak.

He came closer, and she gave a yelp when she felt his fingers on the back of the bodice, tying the tiny fastenings.

'Please don't.'

He ignored her protest and continued to work his way down the bodice. Her spine arched beneath his touch as startling desire mixed with the upset dragging at her throat.

At first his movements were fast, but then he slowed, as though he too was weakened by the tension in the room—the tension of bodies hot and bothered, wanting more, wanting satisfaction.

Finished, he settled one hand on her waist while the other touched the exposed skin of her back above the strapless bodice.

'*Cosa c'e'?* What's the matter?'

She couldn't answer. She longed to pull on her skirt and jumper again. To cover every inch of herself. To not feel so exposed. So vulnerable. So aware of him.

'Look into the mirror, Emma. See how beautiful you are. I wasn't comparing you to models.'

She could not help but laugh. 'God, it's not *that*…it's just.'

His hands twisted her around until she was staring at herself in the mirror.

Sumptuous silk on brittle bones.

She spun back to him, her eyes briefly meeting his before looking away. 'I'm sorry…it's just these dresses remind me of my wedding dress.'

CHAPTER THREE

How could he have been so stupid? Stupid to have agreed to let her work for him. Stupid not to have foreseen how these dresses might remind her of her wedding. Stupid to feel a responsibility towards this stranger. It was all so illogical. He barely knew her. He had too many other problems, responsibilities, in his life. But something about this woman had him wanting to protect her.

His hand moved to touch her, to lift her chin so that he could gaze into her eyes. To offer her some comfort. But he stopped himself in time. She was an employee. She was a runaway bride just burnt in love. He had to keep away from her.

'I will ask Andreina to help you undress. You do not need to try on any more.'

'No. It's okay. I'm sorry…this wasn't supposed to happen.'

He needed to get away. Away from the close confines of this dressing room. Away from how stunningly beautiful she looked in the gown, pale skin against ivory and purple silk. Away from the pain in her eyes he didn't know how to cope with, didn't know how to ease.

'I'll get Andreina.'

Her hand shot out and her fingers encased his wrist. She gave it a tug to halt him. 'Not Andreina. Please will *you* help me untie the bodice?'

Why was she so adamant about Andreina?

He untied the clasps of the bodice, saw her shoulder blades contract into a shrug above the bodice.

'All the dresses are stunning. I would be very proud to wear them. I just need to get used to the idea.'

Her voice shook just like her body.

More than ever he needed to get away.

'Let's talk about it outside.'

He walked out of the fitting room, wanting to get away.

Wanting to go back and take her into his arms.

Five minutes later she joined him outside the store.

Instead of guiding her back to his boat, he led her towards Campo di San Moisè. At the footbridge that led to the square and the baroque façade of Chiesa di San Moisè he found what he was looking for—a street vendor selling *frittelle*, the Venetian-style doughnuts only available during Carnival. He ordered a mixed cone.

They stopped at the centre of the footbridge

and he offered Emma a *frittella* before biting into a *frittella veneziana*. The raisins and pine nuts mixed into the dough were the sugar hit he badly needed.

Emma bit into her *frittella crema pasticcera*, filled with thick custard cream, and gave a little squeal. The custard escaped from the doughnut and dripped down her chin.

Desire, thick and desperate, powered through his body.

They stood in silence, eating the *frittelle*, and he wanted nothing more than to kiss away the grains of sugar glittering on her lips.

The deep upset in her eyes was easing.

He needed to get this over and done with.

'This isn't going to work. I should never have agreed to it.'

She touched her fingers to her mouth and brushed the granules away, heat turning her pale cheeks a hot pink. 'I'm really embarrassed...about getting lost and about what happened in the store. It was unprofessional of me. I promise it won't happen again.'

'You need time to recover from what you have gone through; you shouldn't be working.'

She drank in his words with consternation in her eyes. 'But I need to work—I want to work.'

Why couldn't she see that he was doing her a

favour? That this attraction between them was perilous.

'Why?'

She crumpled the empty *frittella* cone in her hands. 'Because I need the money. Because I want to focus on my career and forget the past year.'

Her jaw arced sideways, as if she were easing a painful tension in her jawline.

'He really hurt you, didn't he?'

Her thick dark eyelashes blinked rapidly, her mouth tensing. She angled away from him to face the canal.

She turned back before she spoke. 'Because of his lies and deception, yes. Because of how he hurt other people.'

How had she not known what he was like? Why had she allowed herself to get hurt like this?

Anger swept through him. Together with the recognition that everything she was going through represented every reason why he would never marry, never give his heart and trust to another person. People always let you down, ultimately.

He had trusted, loved, hero-worshipped Francesco, Marco, Simone, Arnaud, Stefano... All his mother's boyfriends. And they had all walked away from him. Showing just how little significance he'd held in their lives. Blood, family—that was all you could trust in. Nobody else.

'Why were you marrying him?'

She jammed her left heel against the bottom of the bridge rail and rotated her foot. 'You mean why didn't I realise what he was really like? I met him last summer. It was a whirlwind romance. We got engaged after four months. He was charming and outgoing. He seemed to care for me a lot. He worked crazy hours and sometimes he didn't turn up for dates... He always had a plausible excuse and I'd eventually forgive him. When we were together he was kind, if a little distracted...but I never saw the other side to him—the lying, the fraud.'

'Four months isn't a long time to get to know one another.'

Behind them a group of tourists walked by, their guide speaking loudly. Suddenly they all laughed in unison. The guide looked pleased with his joke.

Emma looked at them, taken aback. The tips of her ears were pink from the cold. For a moment he considered giving her his hat. Why did he keep forgetting she was his employee? Was it because they had already lain together in a bed? Even if it had been only for a few crazy minutes of misunderstanding?

She went to speak, but stopped. Her mouth quivered and she looked at him uncertainly. Her chest rose on a deep inhalation. 'I wanted a family of my own...to belong.'

She spoke with such loneliness.

He stamped his feet on the ground. The cold was already stiffening his back. 'Did you love him?'

He had asked the question before he had thought it through. It was none of his business. But he had to know.

Hazel eyes filled with confusion met his for a moment before they fled away. 'Can we not talk about this?'

She was right. But a need to know drove him on to say, 'You must have loved him if you were going to marry him.'

She touched her long slim fingers against her temple and circled them there for a few seconds. The faint impression of a ring recently removed was still there, on the skin of her ring finger. Her eyes scrunched shut. 'I'm not certain of anything any more... Maybe.'

'And what if you had married him but then woke up one morning certain you didn't love him—would you have left?'

She looked at him in horror. 'No. *No*. Absolutely not.'

'Why so certain?'

'I wouldn't just walk away. I take my commitments, my pledges seriously. I don't walk away when things get difficult. Turn my back on someone when things go wrong. I do everything to fix it, to accept where we are.' She threw her head back and looked at him fiercely, her nostrils flaring. 'And, before you say anything, I draw a line at criminality. At months and years of lies and deception. Yes, I walked away from my ex—but I could not stay with a man who had so wilfully hurt so many people.'

She inhaled a breath and her jaw worked. Anger fired in her eyes, and she lobbed a grenade of a question in his direction. 'How about *you*—do you ever want to marry? Have your own family?'

Her grenade exploded in his chest. His stomach clenched at the emotional damage of her question. 'It's not for me—my job, my responsibilities mean I wouldn't be a good husband, a good father. I would be absent too much.'

She considered him for a moment, as though trying to decide if he was a con man too. Slowly she nodded, the anger in her eyes receding. 'That's honourable. Others wouldn't even think to stop and consider whether they would be a good husband and father.'

'There's enough hurt children in this world... I don't want to add to them.'

For a moment he thought he had gone too far. She looked at him questioningly.

But then she stood upright and asked, 'Can I have another chance? I promise no more tears or drama. I would be honoured to wear those dresses. I'll go back and try them on now.'

Back to business. He should end it now.

'Emma, the future of tens of thousands of my employees rest on this trip going smoothly.'

She nodded with a dignified grace, her eyes holding a sombre pride. 'I know. And I respect and understand that. If you firmly believe I'm not right for this position I will walk away.'

Dio! She was good at negotiating.

He checked his watch. 'Lucky for you, I don't have time to argue. I want and need from you complete focus on this client trip. Nothing else. The dresses will all suit you—I'm sure of it. I will have them delivered tomorrow. Now, let's go. I need to get home and change.'

The following evening Emma waited for Matteo out on the terrace, goosebumps of anticipation breaking on her skin. She was accompanying Matteo Vieri to the Venetian opera house, La Fenice. To see Verdi's *La Traviata*. In the opera house in which it had first been performed.

She pulled the belt of her wool-and-angorablend navy coat tighter. The VMV store had delivered it that morning, along with all the other clothes Matteo had selected yesterday.

The past twenty-four hours had passed without incident. No tears on her part. To the clients she presented a sunny face. At times she had even fooled herself into thinking she was coping. But in the quiet moments, when she hadn't been busy, it had all hit her like a *vaporetto* colliding with a gondola.

She still questioned how she had been so blind to her ex's deceit. And any thoughts of the future left her with heart palpitations. And then there was the constant anxiety that she was going to mess up with the clients, with Matteo.

He seemed to be winning over his Chinese clients with a combination of deep respect and vigilant hosting.

She had accompanied the spouses to Murano Island this morning, to view the world-famous glass manufacturing, along with an interpreter and a tour guide, while Matteo and his clients held business meetings. And in the afternoon the entire group had toured the city by gondola.

As Matteo's designated partner, she had accompanied him in the same gondola as the president of the department store chain, Mr Xue, and his wife. It had been oddly intimate, sitting next to him as they had passed under the Rialto Bridge and later viewed the stunning architecture, mosaics and carvings of Basilica di San Marco and the Doge's Palace. He was professorial in his knowledge and passion about both buildings and the history of Venice in general. No wonder he was so successful, with what appeared to be a photographic memory and a charming persona.

Only with her did the charm fade. When they

were alone he was quiet, and she could not help but feel he was keeping his distance from her. Even now she had a strong hunch that he was waiting until the last minute to leave his office for their journey to La Fenice.

She would do anything to take back her behaviour yesterday in the VMV store. She had clearly made him very uncomfortable and it had been totally unprofessional.

Every now and again over the past twenty-four hours she had caught him looking in her direction. He would always look away, but not before a blaze of attraction had surged between them.

'My boat is waiting downstairs for us.'

She turned to find him standing at the terrace doors. 'I'm ready.'

She swallowed the other words that were about to shoot out of her mouth. *You look incredible.* Which was the truth. His dark grey suit jacket skimmed the wide span of his shoulders, and the tailored trousers emphasised the long length of his legs. He shrugged on a long black wool coat, followed by a black wool hat.

As she neared him he handed her a royal blue hat. 'It's cold tonight. You will need to wear some protection.'

The thin-knit hat, the same colour as the appliqué dashes on her navy cocktail dress, had a crystal flower sewn onto it.

Would her heart *please* stop pounding? It was just a practical gesture—nothing else.

'Let me put it on for you. Otherwise your hair might fall down.'

He had to be joking!

But, alas, no. He took the hat from her and delicately pulled it over her hair, which she had coiled up into a tight bun. It was a style she rarely used, for it brought back too many memories of her life as a ballerina. But tonight it had felt apt—not just because it suited the dress but because she needed its severity against how vulnerable she felt about her wedding imploding, the constant stress of worrying if she was doing her job effectively…and her silly, annoying, futile attraction to her boss.

His fingers stroked briefly against the exposed skin of her neck. Her insides melted. He was standing much too close. His scent, his broad chest were too close. His open coat touching against her…too close.

She stepped back. No weakness. Just toughness and protecting herself. That was all that mattered now.

In the darkened theatre, the lovers Violetta and Alfredo begged each other for forgiveness for all the hurt they had caused each other in the past. Their voices soared, their pain and passion for one another holding the crowd transfixed. Alfredo believed that they had a future together, not realising how ill Violetta was...

Matteo could hardly breathe. In his private box, the president of the board, Mr Xue, and his wife were to his right, closest to the stage. Emma was to his left. Because of the way the boxes were angled towards the stage he couldn't see her without turning around. He wanted to turn. He wanted to see if she was okay.

All evening she had done everything possible to make his clients welcome and comfortable. Had been attentive to them at each of the two intervals. But something was wrong. Her body beneath the stunning pencil-fit dark navy dress with dashes of royal blue was too stiff. Her hair, tied up in an elegant bun that matched the knee-length, cap-sleeved gentle decorum of her dress, exposed the tension in her rigid neck.

Violetta fell to the floor. Lifeless.

Behind Mr Xue somebody sniffled.

He had to check.

Her eyes were on the stage. The endless gilt private boxes of La Fenice cascaded behind her. She swallowed hard but did not look in his direction. She was aware of him. He had no doubt about that. Her refusal to meet his eyes sent hot frustration zipping through his muscles. His hands and feet clenched, he shifted in his seat.

The cast moved forward on the stage to take their bows. The crowd stood and shouted their approval. He needed to focus on his clients. But all he was aware of was the exasperatingly beautiful woman next to him.

A woman whose slender waist, small full breasts, high firm bottom and long legs left him with distracted concentration, with a hollow feeling in his stomach, with a desperate compulsion to hold her, kiss her, taste her.

She was an employee. A woman recently heartbroken in love. A runaway bride.

He didn't need any further reasons to stay away from her.

If only his libido would receive that message.

With his clients and their tour guide and interpreter safely aboard the private launch, Matteo watched their boat turning in the water towards the direction of the Hotel Cipriani.

Beside him, Emma quickly yanked the clips from her hair. Thick curls tumbled down her back. Memories of her hair fanned on his pillow the night he'd found her in his bed sent a shock of desire through him. She pulled on her woollen hat, giving him a surreptitious look. The uncomfortable suspicion that she was trying to avoid his help in putting it on set his teeth on edge. He wasn't used to women pushing him away.

Deliberately, he moved closer. Emma gazed up. Startled. But she didn't look away. Her cheeks grew flushed and her eyes darkened, making something explode in his stomach. He adjusted her hat, pulling it down further over her head. And as he held her gaze he ran his fingers down the long length of her hair. He was playing with fire but he didn't care.

He studied her lips in a slow, deliberate drag of his eyes across their plump softness.

Her lips parted and she gave a low, shaky exhalation.

His pulse throbbed at the base of his neck, urging him to taste her, to answer the primitive call aching in his gut, to possess her. To grab her and end this irrational hold she had over him—this foolish, reckless attraction that burned brightly between them.

She stepped back unsteadily. She tugged at the collar of her coat with nervous fingers.

She cleared her throat. 'How are the meetings going?'

He too stepped back. Shook his head, trying to silence the heavy insistent beat of his pulse.

The meetings. He shook his head again. Trying to focus. The meetings. They were going slowly. Which was to be expected. But that did not stop it from being exasperating. All his work over the past few years had been jeopardised by his troubled designer.

The fog of desire slowly lifting, he cleared his own throat. 'Thanks to my designer, I'm having to spend time rebuilding our relationship, re-establishing our respect towards them. They value a long-term relationship rather than a specific deal, and that can't be rushed.'

'What are you going to do about the designer? Will you need to replace him?'

'Trust me, I'm tempted to, and it's what my board would like me to do. But I'm not going to. He has been going through a tough time recently, due to some personal problems. He needs support.'

She gave him a smile that slipped like a pulse of pleasure into his bloodstream. 'Your grandmother isn't the only one with a kind heart.'

'I try to protect my employees, my family...' He paused and swallowed against the sudden kick his heart aimed against his ribs. 'Patrizia—your predecessor—gave birth to a baby boy yesterday afternoon.'

A trace of longing pulled at the corners of her smile. 'That's wonderful news.'

He remembered her words about wanting a family.

Suddenly he wanted to have this night over.

'My boat is waiting for us.'

She gave him a nervous glance before gesturing back towards the city. 'I was thinking of walking back…I haven't seen Venice at night yet.' She took a few steps towards the city. 'I'll see you in the morning.'

She was pushing him away. Annoyance lashed across his skin.

'I'll walk with you.'

His suspicion that she was trying to get away was confirmed by her swift response.

'No! No, I'll walk by myself.'

'Do you know the way?'

'Not really… But I'm sure I'll be fine.'

He threw her an unconvinced look. 'I don't want to have to come and find you in the middle of the night if you get lost, like you did on Giudecca.'

She winced at that. 'I suppose…'

He led her in the direction of Piazza San Marco. They walked in tense silence.

On the narrow Calle Delle Veste, she darted an uncertain look at him before asking, 'Did you grow up in Venice?'

How he wished he *had* grown up in one single place.

'We lived here for a little while. Originally we were from Puglia, in the South. We moved around during my childhood, here in Italy but also in France and Spain.'

'Because of your parents' work?'

Not so much work as where his mother's latest boyfriend had lived. 'There was only my mother and me. Sometimes my grandmother too.'

'So, like me, you had no brothers or sisters.' She said it with a wistfulness that told him she too had dreamed of having some when she was younger. Some allies in life. Someone to talk to.

But then, would he *really* have wanted another child to endure the constant uncertainty of his childhood? The stomach-crunching walk to the door each day after school, wondering if today was the day they were going to pack and leave. Or to be thrown out. The constant fear in the pit of his stomach that his life was going to change again—a new town, a new school, a new man in their lives, but the same isolation, the same insecurity.

They turned into Calle Larga. He pushed away those memories. Only then did he notice how she was struggling to walk.

He slowed down. 'You're limping—are you sure you're okay to walk?'

She waved away his concern with a toss of her hand. 'I'm fine. It's just an old injury that flares up every now and again.'

He slowed his pace even more, unconvinced by her answer. He held out his arm. 'Take my arm.'

She glanced at his arm as though he was offering her something illegal. She bit her lip. But then with a shaky smile she placed her hand on his arm, her elbow tucked beneath his, lightly touching his side.

They walked along the empty *calle*, with Emma slowly placing more weight on his arm. Their steps, at first out of sync, quickly matched each other, and his body hummed, firing with protectiveness for the beautiful, guarded, troubling woman at his side.

Her hand relaxing even more on his arm, she asked, 'Did you mind moving around when you were a child?'

'I hated it.'

Her eyes snapped up to consider him. 'Really?'

'I was always the new boy at school. Sometimes the other children reacted well—I was a novelty. Most of the time, though, I was nothing but a new target.'

She grimaced, her quick shudder rippling against the side of his body. 'You sound as if you were as unhappy in school as I was.'

'What do you mean?'

'I was at ballet boarding school from the age of ten. I adored the ballet—most of the time— but I was lonely.'

'You missed your parents?'

'Yes…sometimes. But I eventually got used to it.'

He knew there was more to it than that, but seeing the closed expression on her face he guessed she didn't want to talk about it.

He decided to change the topic. 'Do you dance now?'

He had hoped to move to neutral territory with his question. But by the crestfallen expression on her face and the way she pulled away from him to walk on her own, without his help, he could see it had obviously backfired.

'No. I haven't danced in years.'

'Why?'

He almost preferred the tears of other times to the stony expression on her face now. Tight, pale lips. The off-kilter edge of upset in her jaw.

He thought she wasn't going to answer, but eventually she said, 'I broke my ankle when I was nineteen. I ended up having to have plates inserted, it was smashed so badly.'

It seemed to have taken a huge effort for her to tell him that much. He should ask no more questions. Leave her be. But he wanted to understand.

'Did it happen whilst you were dancing?'

'Unfortunately not—or maybe fortunately. I was out one night and slipped on wet steps.'

They were once again reaching Campo di San Moisè. The tiny square was empty, and the exuberant exterior of San Moisè church, with its dramatic carved stone, stood like a giant wedding cake awaiting its bride and groom. A lone gondolier floated on the canal below the bridge, his night light briefly flickering over his passengers—a couple entwined. He and Emma stopped at the centre of the bridge and looked down into the water.

Emotion welled in his chest. He wanted to reach out to her. Why, he had no idea. 'Your limping tonight…is that because of the accident?'

Her eyes fixed on the passing boat, she gave a knee-jerk shrug. The shrug of someone who had been pretending for too long. Her hands clasped and tightened the belt of her coat around her narrow waist. She stood on one foot. Flicked the other forward and back.

'Yes, sometimes it acts up. Bad weather or stress seem to particularly aggravate it. The past few days—being questioned by the police, having to call my ex's parents…tell them that the wedding was off—has made it ache like never before.'

She spoke with a hard edge, trying to box off her dismay.

'The past few days have been very difficult for you. I admire how determined you are to move on.'

A sad smile broke on her mouth and her eyes dissolved into soft gratitude. 'Thank you.'

'You were upset tonight.'

Her hand flew to her mouth. 'The clients didn't see, did they? I tried not to…' Her voice trailed off.

'No, they didn't see.'

'But *you* did.'

'I pick up on these things faster than others.'

Which was partially the truth. He had spent his childhood attuned at all times to his mother's mood. Now it was a honed skill that was a powerful tool in the boardroom. But he was especially attuned to Emma. None of his guests tonight would have guessed something was wrong, but he had seen…and felt…the very subtle signs as if they shared a special language all of their own.

Which made no sense. And was deeply, annoyingly, frustratingly unsettling.

'Ballet was my life—'

Her voice cracked and she shut her eyes. When she opened them again they pleaded with him to understand.

'It was everything I'd dreamed of. I was on track to a solo position in the Greater Manchester Metropolitan City Ballet. And suddenly it was all over.'

'You still miss it?'

She gave a hurt laugh, as if she still couldn't believe the awful trick life had played on her.

'Hugely. Tonight…tonight was my first time being inside a theatre since my accident. Over the years I couldn't face being reminded of what I was missing…the thrill as you wait in the wings…the elation at the end of a show. I thought I had come to terms with it, but tonight it was such a beautiful production, such a heartbreaking story…I wished I could have been up there on the stage too.'

'If you miss it so much couldn't you teach, or do something else in the ballet world?'

She touched her hand to her forehead and winced. As if that thought alone caused a headache. 'No, it'd be too hard. I can't go back to it.'

Eyes that knew the pain of loss held his.

Something sharp stabbed his chest.

'Do you dance at *all*?'

She shook her head, looked away. 'I haven't danced since I had my accident, seven years ago.'

'In time you may go back to it—don't totally discount it. From how you describe it, I know it was an important part of your life.'

Her mouth tightened and she blinked hard.

He should suggest they move on.

But he wanted to hold her.

Wanted to see her smile.

Wanted to make things okay for her.

'Will you dance with me now?'

She gazed at him as though he had asked her to scale the outside of the *campanile* in Piazza San Marco. 'Dance with you? Here?'

Okay, so it wasn't something most bosses would suggest to an employee. But then most bosses didn't first encounter an employee by finding them lying in their bed. After that, their relationship was never going to be normal.

'We shared *frittelle* here—why not a dance?'

She looked about her. Taking in where they were properly for the first time. 'I thought the buildings looked familiar.'

He held out his hand to her. 'Well…?'

His hand hung in the air. Long tanned fingers.

Her stomach went into free fall.

She wanted to move towards him.

In that moment his hand seemed like a beacon of escape from reality, if only for a fleeting few minutes.

Boom-boom-boom. Her heart shot up to the base of her throat. Clogging her airways.

But what of her resolution to stay away from men? This attraction was nothing more than a manifestation of her loneliness, her vulnerability. The ultimate rebound fantasy.

But it was all so tempting.

She could lose herself in this intoxicating chemistry between them. Forget about everything that was wrong in her life.

Her hand rose up as though independent of her. Tired of her dithering. Her body was intent on making the decision for her, ignoring all the arguments in her brain.

A sexy, satisfied supernova smile broke on his mouth. He tugged her forward slowly, in no rush. His other hand landed lightly on her waist.

Her hand, her arm, her breast, her neck, her belly and then the entirety of her body was blasted with heat, the surge of something unique.

He began to sway and move them around in circles.

He hummed a low tune.

The tremors in her body lessened.

And then laughter bubbled in her throat and escaped into the chilly night air. She laughed at the craziness of the whole situation. Her. Dancing. With Matteo Vieri. In a deserted square in the most romantic city in the world. And the most surprising, crazy part of it all: he had a deep, beautiful singing voice.

He looked down at her with affectionate amusement.

Their eyes locked. The world slowed down.

They moved closer.

His mouth came close to her ear.

His deep humming moved through her body like a caress.

A hot sensual river seeped through her.

She stepped even closer.

Their bodies met.

She closed her eyes. Light-headed against his scent of powerful musk. At the sensation of being held by him. At their feet moving in unison.

She was *dancing*!

Elation and heartbreak constricted her chest.

Tucked into his side, she felt his hard chest pressed against her breast, his hip against hers.

Want tugged at her core. Leaving her weak-limbed.

She shifted in his arms, her hardened nipples grazing against the press of his chest.

She gave a low gasp.

He moved away from her ear.

She looked up.

His eyes had darkened.

With the same heavy desire she was sure shadowed her own.

His head lowered again. Towards hers. Everything inside her went quiet. His lips hovered over hers. She couldn't keep her eyes open.

His breath, with an intoxicating hint of the brandy he had drunk during the interval, feathered over her skin.

Her lips parted. Felt heavy.

His lips moved against hers softly.

Her mind spun.

With a groan he pulled her closer.

And then she was lost to the warm, masculine sensation of his mouth, to the pressure of his hand on her back, the hardness of his body pushed against hers.

CHAPTER FOUR

WHAT WAS SHE DOING?

Emma pulled away. Breathless. Panic pushing her heart hard. It pounded and crashed in her chest. Physically wounding her.

She was kissing a man. Days after her wedding—her life—had crashed and burned. She was kissing her boss.

For a brief second Matteo looked at her in confusion.

'I'm sorry…that shouldn't have happened,' she said unsteadily.

His eyes hardened and his mouth settled into a tight line of annoyance. He gave a curt nod. 'It's getting late. We should go.'

For a moment she looked at him, at a loss. Wanting more. What, she wasn't sure. But not this awkward, tense, angry, frustrated wall that now stood between them.

They turned and walked through the ancient floating city, the clip of their footsteps mocking the silence between them.

Her body was distracted, acutely aware, on high

alert to the power and strength, the primitive masculine draw of the man walking beside her.

Embarrassment and guilt ate up any words that
tumbled through her brain.

Two days later Emma stared at the event plan for
the reception to be held in Ca' Divina that night
and marvelled at the neatness of the spreadsheet
cells. All so orderly and straightforward. And
nothing like the chaos that had ascended on the
palazzo since early that morning.

She ticked off the box for reconfirming the private launches that would transport the guests to
Ca' Divina.

If only she was able to place a satisfying, ten-
sion-releasing tick in all the other empty boxes
winking up at her, taunting her with their blank-
ness. The caterers, the audio-visual team, lighting and florists were still setting up. They were
supposed to have finished over an hour ago.

In her stomach anxiety popped like popcorn
kernels. She pushed her hand sharply against
her belly. A warning not to give in to her own
self-doubts. She had this under control. The reception *would* be a success. Matteo's clients,
his A-list celebrity guests and all the local digni-
taries would be suitably impressed. Matteo would
be impressed.

And maybe then the awful tension that had

sprung up between them since they had danced and kissed in San Moisè Square would ease. It was a tension that had seen them talking to one another uneasily, maintaining a ridiculous physical space at all times when they were in the same room, as if standing too close might be dangerous.

Something huge, awkward and unsaid was dangling between them.

Dancing with him had been wondrous, but his strength and care had made her feel even more vulnerable, more susceptible to him.

Raised voices down on the landing stage had her standing up from where she had been working at the dining table out on the terrace and walking to the balustrade.

Matteo was home.

An hour earlier than she'd expected.

He was exchanging terse words with one of the lighting electricians whilst gesturing furiously at some electrical cables lying along the landing stage.

She grabbed her file and ran through the terrace doors, out into the huge central room filled with stunning frescos that she had learned from Matteo was called a *portego*, and down the wide marble stairs that led to the water gate.

Head down, Matteo charged up towards her. They met halfway.

Anxiety and attraction mixed explosively in her heart, which was about to *jeté* right out of her chest.

Stern brown eyes flaring with coppery tints flicked over her. '*E'tutto pronto per sta sera?* Is everything ready for tonight?'

Her professional smile wavered. And she wanted to weep. Because she wanted nothing more than to step closer. Lay her hand on his arm. Touch the wool of his coat.

Did *he* suffer any of this intense chemistry that made her feel constantly faint?

Did *he* think of their kiss?

Did *he* want, like she did, to have the world sing and shine and sizzle again?

Did *he* spend hours driving himself crazy, thinking about it…and then spend the rest of the day berating himself for thinking such crazy, impossible, self-destructive thoughts?

Probably not.

She clasped the file even tighter in her hand, her nails—French-polished for the wedding—digging into the soft cardboard. 'Everything is on track to be ready…the set-up is just taking a little longer than planned.'

With an impatient sigh he turned away and climbed the stairs at a jog.

She ran after him, cursing the twinge in her ankle.

He stopped at the first room he came to—the cosy and inviting writing room.

Inside, the staff hired to act as cloakroom attendants were still packing the gift boxes that would be given to each guest on departure. They had set up an impressive production line on top of a matching pair of painted credenzas. Skincare products, perfumes and designer sunglasses—all from Matteo's lines—were being placed into exquisite ballet-slipper-pink boxes printed with hundreds of tiny gold VMV logos.

With a shake of his head Matteo turned away.

In the *portego*, he stopped and looked critically at the florists, who were finishing off a huge globe centrepiece filled with pretty roses the same pink as the gift boxes—the signature colour of VMV.

'Isn't it beautiful?'

He didn't respond, but stared critically at the endless cuttings and the florists' paraphernalia on the floor, needing to be tidied away.

In the ballroom he stalked about the double-height room like a matador awaiting the release of the bull. He glared at the audio-visual technician, still setting up, and then rearranged some of the gilded furniture which had been moved to the corners of the room to allow the guests to circulate easily.

Emma bit back on her impulse to ask him to

stop, to inform him that she had arranged the furniture in such a pattern deliberately. Instead she said, 'The catering manager and I will be briefing the waiting staff in five minutes. The head of security will be here soon with his team. I will also have a briefing meeting with him.'

Matteo made no comment, but strode out onto the terrace. Emma guessed she was expected to follow.

When she came alongside him he stabbed a finger down towards the water. 'Why is there no red carpet on the landing stage?'

She flicked open her folder. Nobody had said anything about a red carpet. Had she missed it in the schedule? Frantically she scanned the document.

'I didn't know there was supposed to be one. Shouldn't it be pink, anyway? To keep it in line with the pink VMV theme of the evening?'

He looked at her with a puzzled frown for a second. Then he said, in a slow *I'm trying to control my temper here* voice, 'Just sort it out.'

He turned and stabbed his finger at the terrace table.

'And sort out that mess on the table.'

'Of course.'

'Do you *always* work in such chaos?'

Okay, so she had left some files and paperwork on the table when she had rushed to meet him.

But nothing that warranted such a damning tone. Why was he trying to pick a fight with her?

'Is everything okay?'

For a brief second he looked taken aback by her question, but then that hard Roman emperor jawline tensed. 'Why shouldn't it be?' He didn't wait for her to answer but instead demanded, 'Is the photographer here?'

Why did he have to home in on everything that was going wrong with the plan? 'His flight was delayed. He'll be here in the next hour.'

He walked away from her, but turned at the terrace door. 'I'll be in my office. Send the head of security in to me when he arrives. *I'll* manage his briefing. The same with the photographer.'

Unease prickled at the top of her spine. She rolled her head, but a million tiny pinpricks of pressure persisted. Why was he trying to take over her responsibilities?

'There's no need. I have everything under control.'

He yanked off his outer coat and tossed it under his arm. His light grey suit jacket was open and it flared back to give her a glimpse of his powerful torso, flat stomach, narrow hips. Hips that had crushed against her two nights ago.

Desire spun within her—coiling, whipping, hollowing out her insides.

Her hips, her skin, her mouth suddenly wanted

him. Wanted his strength. Wanted the undoing effect of his scent. Wanted the feverish pull of his dazzling fingers trailing across her skin.

His expression hardened. 'But that's the problem. You clearly haven't. The *palazzo* is a mess. Nothing is ready. I'm disappointed. I expected better.'

His words sliced through her.

Through her crazy physical draw to him.

Through her pride.

Through all the promises she had made to herself that she was going to be tough, that she was going to stand up for herself.

'The *palazzo* will be ready. Within the next hour. The guests aren't arriving for another three hours.'

She tilted her head and, despite her mouth feeling like two rigid lines frozen in place, dug out a smile.

'I think you should have belief in me and the rest of the crew.'

Her short-lived smile collapsed, and she didn't care that it was replaced with a scowl.

He tossed his coat onto his other arm and stepped back out onto the terrace. His eyes were dark, dark, dark, as if his every feeling towards her had sucked any light out of them.

'You have to earn my belief first, and so far you're not doing a very good job.'

* * *

The corridor down to his office was blocked by two waiters carrying a long wooden table in the direction of the lounge. A lightning glare sent them scurrying away. In his haste, the waiter at the back drove a table leg into the calf of the waiter carrying the table at the front. The waiter grimaced hard, but avoided looking in Matteo's direction. Keen to get away.

A shade of guilt accompanied Matteo into his office.

He flung open his laptop. Impatience clung to him. Did it *always* take so long for the laptop to power up?

His clients were stalling. The contracts should have been signed today. For the first time ever he was unable to read his clients, to assess what their negotiation tactics were. Were they still unsure about the relationship? Unsure about the trust and respect between them? Or were they looking to gain an advantage in the contract negotiations?

It felt as though his negotiation instincts had been knocked off course. Nothing had been the same since Tuesday night. When he had danced with Emma. Had held her slight frame in his arms. Had kissed her soft mouth. When nothing had ever felt so right. When in truth it was all wrong.

She had pulled away.

Rightly so.

But that didn't mean it hadn't stung. She had looked aghast. Even now his ego felt affronted by her horror.

He hated how attracted he was to her. How he constantly thought about her. The eternal distraction of her.

He should have been the one to pull away. She was an employee. Living in his home. A bruised runaway bride, no doubt messed up and confused. He hadn't acted honourably. That was what stung the most.

Finally the email icon popped up on his laptop.

He leaned forward in his chair and clicked on a New York Fashion Week update from the head of PR with VMV.

A hot dart of pain stung the base of his spine. He closed his eyes. *Dio!*

Tonight *had* to go smoothly. Thousands of his employees were depending on him. This business was his life, his everything. What would he be without it?

Tonight he was about to reveal his final bargaining chip to secure the deal with his clients. A promise that the globe's hottest celebrity couple, Hollywood stars Sadie Banks and Johnny North, would open his collections at the Chinese clients' flagship stores in Hong Kong and Beijing.

Sadie and he had dated years ago, and had kept

in contact for business purposes. She and Johnny were both going to attend the reception tonight. Their first appearance since their surprise marriage a fortnight ago, conducted in complete secrecy with only immediate family and friends in attendance. Sadie had worn a VMV gown.

Denied shots of the wedding, the media and public would be clamouring for a photo. Which, of course, would be taken with the president of China's most prestigious department store chain standing in between them.

The reception needed to be relaxed, slick, effortless. Everything it currently wasn't.

A knock sounded on his door. Before he had the opportunity to respond Emma entered and introduced a short, intent-looking man. The head of security.

Matteo gestured for the man to sit. Emma sat next to him, across the desk from Matteo.

Her hair was tied back in a ponytail, and she wore a white blouse with thin aqua-blue strips, a wide bow on the high collar. Beneath: dark navy tailored trousers. Her only obvious make-up was a deep red lipstick on her generous cupid's bow lips. Desire hit him hard. For a moment he could only stare at her. His fingers itching to undo each tiny pearl button running down the front of her blouse.

She was the cause of his negotiating instincts

being off course. *She* was to blame. She had asked him earlier to believe in her. He had learned a long time ago not to trust in anyone but himself. That was not going to change any time soon—especially with a woman who had such a disturbingly bewitching effect on him.

Frustration wrapped around his throat. 'Emma, I will handle this.'

Ignoring him, she twisted to face the head of security, flinging her head back defiantly. She delivered a killer smile to the man, whose focused demeanour crumbled into a smitten gaze.

She passed him a file. 'This is an updated list of guests. Prince Henri is no longer able to attend.'

Matteo sat back in his chair as Emma continued to brief the security head. Anger fused with his earlier desire. Tension leached into his muscles. He forced himself to maintain restraint. Until he got her alone.

He couldn't fault her performance. She provided the head of security with every key piece of information he needed and easily answered all his questions.

But he *could* fault her insubordination. Her intrusion into his life. He *could* fault his own absurdity in feeling things for this woman that had him unable to concentrate in meetings. That had him craving the opportunity to spend time with her, to talk with her, to touch her, to taste the exhilarating heat of her mouth again.

Ten minutes later the meeting was wrapped up. The head of security provided Matteo with reassurances that, together with assistance from the local *carabinieri*, his team would be able to handle any potential security issues.

Emma walked to the office door with the security head. She offered Matteo a brief nod. Throughout the meeting she had held his gaze resolutely whenever he'd addressed her. He had deliberately pinned her with a furious stare. Wanting to see contrition in her eyes. Contrition for not obeying his orders. Contrition for turning his life upside down from the moment he'd found her lying in his bed.

'Emma, please wait.'

She stood by the open door as the security head walked away.

Music floated on the air. The string quartet rehearsing in the lounge.

For a moment he couldn't speak—couldn't break away from the powerful beauty of her hazel eyes. The soft, tender, romantic music wrapped around his heart—and then frustration hurled through him again. He gritted his teeth against his own insanity.

'Close the door.'

She did as he asked, but stayed at the now closed

door, her shoulder hugging the edge of the door frame.

'I said that *I* would handle the briefing with the security head.'

Her body gave a start at the anger in his voice but then she stood upright, tilting her head back to gaze at him. 'It's okay. I was free and I had the most up-to-date guest list.'

'No. It *isn't* okay. I said that I didn't need you.'

Perspiration was breaking out on Emma's skin.

Her heart was banging a slow booming beat in her chest while the soulful melodies of Shostakovich's 'Romance Theme from The Gadfly' continued to seep under the closed door. Adding to her sense of foreboding.

She had guessed that Matteo wouldn't be happy with her leading the briefing. But she hadn't bargained on the alarming fury in his eyes. The dangerous coiled energy pulsating from his every pore.

Logic and her heart teamed up to beg her not to speak. Not to ask the one question boiling in her stomach.

But her new-found reckless defiance didn't heed them. 'Are you like this with *all* your employees?'

Her heart thundered in disbelief that she said those words out loud. She took small consolation from the fact that she hadn't also asked if it was only with her that he acted so harshly. *Because of their kiss.* Did he regret it so much? Was he determined to push her away?

'When I need to be.'

'Matteo.' Her throat tightened even at saying his name. Regret punched her gut. But then anger overtook her. Anger that she was so drawn to this man. Anger that all her pledges to toughen up, to protect herself, had been nothing but empty promises.

She stepped away from the door. 'You employed me to do a job. Please let me do it.'

'Are you always this obstinate?'

'No. And unfortunately I have paid dearly as a result.'

'Meaning?'

'I allowed my ex to convince me that a short engagement was the right thing, when in truth I wanted more time. I allowed my mother and father to push me, to control every part of my life.'

She paused, emotion caught in her throat. She wanted to turn around and walk out of his office. Away from the hardness in his eyes. She didn't know where her throat ended and her heart began. Both were aching…a continuous fault line in her chest.

'I should have pushed for what I wanted and

maybe then they would have had more respect for me.'

He folded his arms. His jaw tightened.

He looked down at his desk.

He unfolded his arms.

He pressed the metal of one cufflink. And then the other.

He prodded some paperwork.

He looked back up, his gaze trailing over the wall behind her, inhaled deeply.

He looked at her briefly and then gestured to the chair where she had earlier been seated. 'Sit down.' He stopped and exhaled a lungful of irritation. 'Sorry, *please* sit down.'

The second time around his voice was more conciliatory. Less harsh. Almost like the voice of the Matteo who had taken her in his arms the other night.

She sat, but kept her mask of imperturbability firmly on. She held his gaze, refusing to acknowledge the horrible vulnerability stirring in her stomach.

'I do respect you.'

She raised a single eyebrow.

He continued. 'Tonight *has* to go well. The clients are refusing to sign. Tonight I have to persuade them to do so. I expect that when they meet Sadie Banks, who is a brand ambassador for VMV, they will fully appreciate the mutual benefits of our alliance.'

Fresh unease grabbed hold of her stomach at the thought of all the sophisticated guests attending the reception. What on earth was she going to speak to them about?

'What role do you want me to play tonight at the reception?'

He drew a hand across his face, his long fingers brushing against his lips. Tired. Puzzled. Weary. 'You're my co-host, as with all the other events. Why would it be any different?'

The vulnerability chilling her bones, setting her on edge, had her speaking out, needing to understand where she stood with him. 'After Tuesday night I wasn't sure.'

He shifted in his seat. 'That obviously was a mistake.'

A mistake?

She knew it was. But hearing him say it in such a cold, dispassionate tone was like a slap.

'Yes, it was.' She gave him a polite smile, despite the anger propelling through her, making her want to snarl instead. 'I think they call it a rebound kiss.'

His jaw worked. And then a cruel smile crept onto his mouth. '*Cara*, we both know that was a lot more than a rebound kiss.'

His voice, dangerous but laced with sexy appeal had her shooting out of her chair. 'I must go and check if the photographer has arrived.'

Matteo gave a low curse. He felt as though his stomach had sunk down to the bottom of the canal.

He slammed shut the lid of his laptop. What was the matter with him? Why was he playing mind games with her?

He called to her retreating back. 'Being with anyone is a bad idea for you right now…especially someone like me.'

She twisted around. 'Like you?'

'I date women, Emma, but I'm not interested in anything serious. My longest relationship lasted less than six months. I have never even lived with a woman. I'm not interested in the emotions and demands of a relationship.'

Her mouth pursed indignantly. 'Do you *really* think that I want to be in a relationship? After everything I've gone through? I want to be on my own, to be independent, create my own life. I'm not trusting a man again for as long as I live.'

'But you said the other day you wanted a family.'

'Well, I can't have one now, can I?'

The thought of her with another man stuck in his throat like a bite-size canapé, but he forced himself to say, 'Not all men are like your ex. In time you'll meet someone else.'

She threw her eyes heavenwards, as though he was trying her patience. 'I'm not interested.'

Somewhere deep within him longing stirred. His stomach clenched at the way it grabbed his heart. Without thinking he said, 'Give yourself time. I can see you with lots of *bambini*.'

'I really don't think so.' She spoke with a dispassionate tone but her eyes told the truth of her vulnerability.

A vulnerability that was uncomfortably familiar.

He knew he should shut down this conversation. That he was single-handedly pulling them both into dangerous territory. But something inside him needed to know. Needed to know if it had hurt her as much as it had him to be rejected.

'On that first night you said you have no family. What did you mean?'

She considered him for a moment and then said starkly, 'When I was no longer able to dance my parents made it clear that they no longer wanted me in their lives.'

'Why?'

'Because they blamed me for ruining everything.'

'Ruining what?'

'Their dreams of having a daughter who was a world-famous ballet star. I told them time and time again that that had never been going to happen, even if I hadn't got injured. I was a good ballet dancer, but I was never going to make it onto the world stage… They persisted in thinking otherwise.'

'And just because you couldn't dance they pushed you away?'

She gave a dispassionate shrug. 'Yes, and it's understandable. They spent years supporting me financially. They both worked two jobs to put me through ballet school. They had no life other than ballet—the endless rehearsals and auditions, travelling to see me perform. Supervising me stretching in the evenings. Repairing my kit. They sacrificed everything. And I let them down.'

'It was an accident.'

'I know. But to them it was the end of the world.'

Defiant hazel eyes held his, but her voice and her lips, too tightly marshalled, told another story. One of pain and bewilderment.

And Matteo realised he had never felt so undone.

In the past he had always effortlessly moved women in and out of his life with words full of charm and regret. But for some reason he wanted to help Emma. Even knowing that to do so would be dangerous, that he should be keeping his distance, not becoming desperate to know her better, to wipe away the fear and anxiety that were now flooding her eyes.

'But your parents, the accident, your wedding… none of what went wrong is your fault. You're so matter-of-fact about it all. Aren't you angry?'

'Matteo, you're my boss. Why are we talking about this? What does it matter?'

'Just because I'm your boss doesn't mean that I can't be human.'

She arched an eyebrow at that.

He touched the platinum of his cufflinks. Cleared his throat and said, 'Life has been pretty unfair to you recently.'

'I can cope on my own.'

Her defiant tone had him demanding, 'So is that why you are staying here?'

She didn't answer—just looked away, her mouth twisting unhappily.

'Can you reconnect with your parents? Is that an option?'

She leaned back against the wall beside the door with a tired exhalation. 'No. After my accident I thought that maybe with time they would adjust. Accept what had happened. I'd send cards for their birthdays, for Christmas, but they would just send them back unopened.'

'Why were they so unforgiving? It was an *accident*.'

Her eyes moved upwards to the eighteenth-century frescoed ceiling, a blush the same colour as her lipstick appearing on her cheeks. 'Because

I had had a glass of wine the night I fell down the steps at the nightclub I was in. They chose to believe that I was drunk. When I wasn't. They blamed me for going out. For choosing to spend time with my friends rather than focusing exclusively on my ballet.'

How could they have turned her away? Their own flesh and blood.

'They should have put you first—your happiness. That should be every parent's priority. What about your friends? Were they able to help?'

'My friends back then were supportive at first…' Her hand moved up and drifted across her neck, her fingers tapping against her skin. 'But they were all in the ballet world. I drifted away from them eventually. It was too hard for everyone. I could see their guilt when they spoke about ballet in front of me…'

For the first time since she had entered his office she looked at him with total honesty, no artificial mask of hardness.

'And it tore me apart.'

Her sadness filled the room with the stinging effect of invisible tear gas.

His throat stung…his chest felt heavy.

He suddenly wished he had been there for her. Had known her when she was nineteen. Had known her even earlier. Had been able to protect her from life's unfairness.

She closed her eyes for a few seconds, her face tightening into a wince. 'I just wish I'd stood up to my parents, to my ex.'

'What do you mean?'

Instead of answering she glanced uncertainly towards the chair where she had earlier been seated. She edged back towards it and sat. Her eyes fixed on to a point over his shoulder, she said, 'I had a very intense relationship with my parents. I was an only child. There was a lot of expectation. I always wanted to please them. But even when I was selected at a competition or an audition, and I looked out at them in the audience…I knew that on the way home they would only talk about the next audition, how to get me to the next level. The extra classes they would organise. The money they were saving to send me to ballet school.'

'That was a lot of pressure for a child.'

'I guess…I loved dancing so much…but it was lonely. I was never allowed to spend time with my friends. When the neighbourhood children knocked on the door for me to come out and play my mother would refuse to let me go. I thought ballet boarding school would change all that…and it did eventually—I made some good friends— but for the first few years I was homesick.'

She tilted forward in her chair and squeezed both knees with her hands. Tight. Memories were causing a line of tension to dissect her forehead.

'At some auditions my mum used to be really nasty about the girls she saw as my rivals. People would overhear—it was horrible. I tried to get her to stop but she wouldn't… It was so embarrassing. And unfair. The other girls thought that I was the same as her; it took a long time before they realised I wasn't. I never stood up to my parents because I was frightened that they would take away what I loved so much. My ballet lessons. The funding for the ballet school.'

She looked down towards her feet. Not looking up, she gave a shrug while her body tilted ever so slightly forward and back, propelled by the movement of her feet.

'Being on stage was magical. In the rehearsals, in ballet class, I would lose myself to the beauty of the movements. Even when I was injured and struggling, ballet gave me life. Happiness.' She looked up suddenly, her eyes sparking with anger. 'But if I had been brave enough to get past my fear of upsetting my parents—been tougher and pushed for what I wanted—told them that I didn't want them controlling every aspect of my life— maybe they would have backed off, become less obsessed. Not have been so devastated when it all came to a crashing end.'

'You can't blame yourself for their reaction to the accident.'

She gave a *you don't understand* sigh. 'It was the same with my ex. Maybe if I'd said no to him, that I wanted a longer engagement… So many people wouldn't be hurt. Now his poor parents have not only his embezzlement to deal with but also the embarrassment of the wedding being called off on the day of the ceremony. They had invited over a hundred of their friends. They're lovely people… His mum was so happy about us marrying. They were both so proud of him.'

'You're not to blame.'

'But what about my behaviour? I didn't rock the boat, say no, stand up to my parents, because I wanted to stay in ballet. I didn't tell my ex that I didn't want a rushed wedding because I wanted a family of my own so badly. I was so damn *passive* in it all. I refused to listen to my own doubts about marrying him. Was I putting my own happiness in front of what was right for my parents? For my ex? Was I complicit in things going so badly wrong? I should have been stronger, tougher.'

CHAPTER FIVE

MATTEO SPRANG FROM his chair, hating to hear her blame herself. 'You had the right to want those things. A career in ballet and…'

Pain shot from his spine down into his glutes.

He lowered his head and gave a low curse.

'And a family.'

His heart began to pound unaccountably and he found it difficult to speak.

'Nobody would blame you for wanting those things.'

He turned away from her cool shrug to look out of the window.

Soft, decadent Botticelli clouds hung over the red-tiled rooftops and the endless church domes and *campaniles* of Venice, pausing at the will of the unpredictable breeze to dance before the sun.

He had long ago accepted he would never have a family of his own. He never wanted to have his heart ripped in two ever again. Why, then, did it sadden and disturb him so much to talk about family with Emma?

'It doesn't matter anyway. It's all in the past.'

He turned around at her words. The clipped, clear tone was not really her voice.

'Now I just want to focus on my future, on being truly independent. I'm tired of being answerable to others. I want a career I can be proud of. And I'm going to fight for it.'

'By fighting me?'

'Not fighting you. Standing up to you. Because I'm good at my job, Matteo. And I want to be a new me. More independent…I want to be hard-headed and resilient.'

'I'm no pushover.'

'Good.' She stood and walked to the door. 'And now that we understand one another, the first thing I'm going to do is show you some Pilates stretches for your back.'

Puzzled, he said, 'My back?'

She cast a critical gaze over him. 'It's obviously hurting you. What caused it?'

'I was sailing last summer, and after I'd winched in a sail in heavy seas it felt a little tighter…it's been bothering me ever since.'

'What has your doctor said about it?'

'Nothing. I haven't had the time to visit him.'

She shook her head, disappointed in him.

He stood a little straighter. He took care of himself physically. He didn't need Pilates. 'Thanks for the offer, but I have business to take care of.'

She threw him a challenging gaze. 'Now, let's

not have a stand-off over this. You've said that tonight is important to you. I know how energy-sapping pain is. Let me show you some exercises that might ease yours. Less pain will allow you to enjoy tonight more and concentrate better.'

She didn't wait for his answer, but spoke as she walked towards the door. 'There isn't enough room in here. Follow me upstairs. The floor space in one of the bedrooms will be perfect.'

A little while later, lying on an antique rug in the *sala azzurra*—the blue bedroom—staring up at the Virgin-blue ceiling, Matteo couldn't decide if he had lost his mind or whether it was rather enjoyable to be lying beside Emma. Pretending to listen to her instructions when in truth his concentration was shot to pieces because she kept touching him.

So much for keeping her at arm's length.

'Now that you have your chin, shoulder blades, arms, pelvis and feet correctly positioned, we will start with a basic move: the leg slide.'

Sitting up beside him, while he remained lying on the floor, with his legs bent, she moved her hands once again onto his hips and applied a gentle pressure. He swallowed a groan.

'Remember to keep a neutral pelvis position.'

Dio! Had she *any* idea what it was like to have her so close? To have her fingers touching him?

'Now, on an inhale slide your right leg out until it's fully extended, and on an exhale pull it back into position.'

He did as she said.

She lay down next to him. 'Good—now do the same with the left leg.'

He followed her count for drawing alternate legs in and out. Next he drew alternate arms back to reach behind him, with Emma all the time telling him to focus, to maintain a neutral position. To breathe.

This was a workout his *nonnina* would enjoy.

'Are you sure that these exercises are of use?'

'Absolutely. They're a major part of any dancer's life and I still practise Pilates every day. It strengthens your core and it's vital in recovery from injury. These exercises are hugely beneficial to people with back pain.'

They finished the arm extensions and Emma sat up. 'The exercises will help, but you need to visit your doctor too.'

'I will after this week.'

'You *could* say it with a little more conviction.'

'I'm busy.'

She tucked her feet underneath her bottom, her crossed legs folding easily into a yoga position. She leaned towards him. 'Being stressed is a major cause of back problems.'

'I'm not stressed.'

She folded her arms and gave him a *who are you trying to kid?* look. 'Stress always aggravates my ankle. Why is the China deal so important to you?'

He shuffled on the ground, suddenly uncomfortable lying in such a vulnerable position. 'Can we just focus on the exercises, please…? The photographer will be here soon.'

She studied him for a moment, but then with a shrug said, 'Fine—let's move on to the bridge exercise.'

She instructed him on the movements needed with her hand touching his stomach. The gentle weight burnt through the cotton of his shirt. Her little finger rested on the silver buckle of his belt.

Dio!

'Remember to keep your pelvis neutral. And *breathe.* You're not breathing!'

What did she expect? He was having to lie there pretending that his body *wasn't* a heat-seeking missile about to launch. Having to fight every instinct that was yelling at him to intercept those torturous touches and pull her down on top of him and kiss her for the next fortnight.

Why hadn't he just said that this wasn't working earlier in his office? That having her live here in Ca' Divina was akin to torture? Knowing that she was lying in her bed at night, only a few doors away… A thought that had kept him awake, pacing the terrace into the early hours every night.

He was even more out of control than Ettore's head designer.

Her hand pressed a little more firmly. 'Now, one vertebra at a time, sink your spine down to the ground.'

He needed to speak. To distract himself.

'I need the Chinese clients to sign because many of our other major markets are contracting due to recessions and political instability.'

She lay down beside him once again and silently indicated that he should follow her lead in pulling his left leg in towards his body and then his right leg. She hugged her own legs with a graceful flexibility.

He gazed back up at the ceiling. She would never dance in a ballet again. How incredible it would have been to see her dance.

Without looking, he knew she was staring directly at him. His heart slowed as beautiful dread moved through him.

Why was she getting to him so much? Why did he feel such a thumping connection with her?

His gaze blended with hers. And despite himself he smiled at her. Wanting to reach out.

Rosy-cheeked, she smiled back. That smile touched something inside him every time she punched him with it. And then her gaze whooshed away. As if she had been caught unawares.

The door to the bedroom was slightly ajar. From downstairs he could hear the quartet rehearsing. The sound of raised voices. But it felt as though they were alone in a cocoon of connectedness. Of understanding. With the early spring sun warming the room.

Her hands were clasped together on her stomach, as if in prayer. Her lips worked for a while before she spoke. 'What might happen if they don't sign?'

Just like that the peace of a few moments ago was shattered. His fear for the business fused with his fear about what was happening between them.

'Worst-case scenario: I'll have to shut down some operations. Consolidate. Which will put people out of work.'

'That upsets you?'

He had been about to stand up. He needed to walk out the tension in his body. Move away from the power she exerted over him. But her question, so quietly asked, so full of softly spoken understanding, had him looking back into eyes that practically swallowed him up with empathy.

'I set up my factories in areas with significant unemployment and poverty. People will struggle to find alternative employment. I put years of training into giving them the skills required. They depend on me.'

'You gave them skills—skills they can bring to other employers.'

'Yes, but there *aren't* employers in those areas.'

'But having so many skilled workers might attract new employers into the area. Maybe some of your staff will go on and set up their own companies. Whatever happens, it doesn't have to be the end. There's always another solution.'

Taken aback by her arguments, by the fact that she was challenging him, he considered them for a moment in silence. And quickly dismissed them. She didn't understand his level of responsibility to so many people. Already irritated, he felt a spark of annoyance as a truth he had been ignoring flamed into life when he thought further about her words.

'Am I the solution to *your* current situation?'

She stared at him, her mouth silently opening and closing. 'Are you asking me if I'm using you?'

'*Are* you?' he shot back, vocalising the hurt and frustration coiling in his body.

She looked away and stared up at the ceiling. 'What have I done to make you think that?'

Her voice was low, resigned. The voice of someone who wasn't surprised by his unfair question. The voice of someone who was used to being disappointed by others.

Guilt tore through him. 'I'm sorry.'

'Do you want me to leave?'

Above him, the Murano glass of the bedroom chandelier swayed slightly as a breeze blew through the ajar door.

He should say yes.

He shouldn't be lying here with her, distracted from his responsibilities.

He shouldn't be feeling so attracted—*Dio*, so innately connected—to a woman who had been so recently hurt.

But all those shouldn'ts failed to cancel out his desire to spend time with her. 'I want you to stay.'

She nodded to this. And then her entire body gave a shudder.

She was shaking off his earlier words.

Shaking *him* off.

He sat up. Needing to put this right.

She looked at him warily.

'I'm cautious about who I let into my life.'

At first she nodded, but then she sat up too. Her head bent, she ran her fingers over the blue and ivory motifs on the rug. 'I can understand why... I would be too, in your position.'

She looked at him with solemn eyes, filing away another piece of information on him. And then a small smile broke on her mouth.

It grew even wider.

She gave a giggle which danced into his heart.

She toppled sideways, reaching out a hand to the rug to steady herself.

Vibrant. Elegant. Fairy-tale pretty.

'Finding me in your bed must have been a huge shock!'

He found himself grinning alongside her. 'It was a most unusual homecoming present.'

She tilted towards him, amusement lighting up her face. 'I've never seen myself as a *present*.'

Her voice was light, playful, teasing.

'A beautiful, distracting present to keep me sane this week.'

Why was he talking to her like this? Why did he have an unstoppable urge to flirt with her? To see her smile and laugh.

'I'm glad I have my uses.'

They sat and smiled at each other.

Foolishly, light-heartedly, soul-enhancingly.

Life buzzed in his veins.

A door closed downstairs.

His fingers tingled with the urge to reach out, to place his hand on her bent knee, to connect physically with her.

To untie the bow at the neck of her blouse…to curl her hair between his fingers.

To kiss her. To have some fun. To know her better.

Her smile slowly faded. And was eclipsed by eyes full of questions and longing.

The same longing that was banging in his chest.

Longing which filled the cavity of space that separated them.

He needed to get them back on solid ground. To establish the nature of their relationship. To stop flirting with her.

'You know, my back *does* feel better. But we need to go downstairs... You should be supervising.'

It took a few seconds for the giddiness in her belly to dissolve and for reality to take its place. He was her boss. She had to protect herself. Stop allowing her physical attraction to him overrule all logic.

He had taken off his jacket when they had come upstairs and draped it on the back of a chair. He had also reluctantly removed his tie and shoes, at her suggestion. He sat before her, his legs bent and crossed, almost matching her lotus position. She was desperately trying not to stare at the powerful strength of his thighs, the captivating narrowness of his hips, the broadness of his chest beneath his white shirt. He dominated the room.

A question was twisting and twisting in her airway, being driven upwards by the unease flapping in her stomach like a hundred butterflies trying to escape.

'Is this going to work?'

The soft espresso warmth of his gaze moved to the coolness of coffee *gelato*.

'It can work if we are both clear that this is a *business* relationship. Two colleagues working together for another few days.'

She wanted to ask what would happen at the end of the week. Would they ever see each other again?

But how on earth was that going to work? A billionaire retail legend and a marketing assistant…a runaway bride.

He studied her, waiting for her to speak.

And the puzzle in her brain as to how they could possibly be just colleagues was constantly jumbled by her glances at him. Thick dark eyebrows were drawn in, there was an evening shadow on his golden jawline, his wide mouth set in neutral…all waiting, waiting, waiting. Waiting for her to speak. But all she could think of was how much she wanted to run her fingertip across that jawline, down his powerful neck, along the topography of his shoulders.

The chemistry between them was about to burn her up. She had never before met a man who literally took her breath away with his looks alone.

Maybe they *could* be colleagues for this week. And in years to come she would look back on the week she'd spent in Venice with this most beautiful man with hopefully fond memories. And her heart intact.

Being his colleague and having the professional friendship that entailed she could just about handle.

Anything more would be devastating.

So it was time she put her 'colleague' mask on and ignored the way her body was screaming out for him like a truculent toddler in the sweet aisle of a supermarket.

'Colleagues need to be honest with one another—do you agree?'

Cautiously he answered, 'It depends…'

She shot him a challenging look. 'I've told you about my parents, my past…things I have never spoken about before.'

His eyes narrowed suspiciously. 'Okay…what's your point?'

'I have a question. When you've accomplished so much, why are you so tough on yourself? I've seen the light on in your office late into the night. You work so hard. Why are you so driven? So worried about the future?'

He rested a hand behind him on the rug and leaned back, considering her question. His silver belt buckle winked up at her. *Remember me? Remember how it felt to touch the hard muscles of this stomach?* No unengaged abdominal muscles there. Just firm muscles layered below hot skin.

Her eyes darted up to where he had undone his top button. Golden skin called to her. She inhaled a deep breath, her insides collapsing into a puddle of desire.

'Because I have people dependent on me—my employees, my family. I have responsibilities that *demand* that I worry, take nothing for granted. Anticipate the worst.'

His words and his serious tone pulled her out of her visual voyage of discovery. Immediately she felt guilty. What type of colleague was she? To be distracted by the superficial when he was telling her something so important?

'That's a whole load of responsibility for one man to carry.'

His eyes held hers and whipped open her soul. Even before he spoke her heart began to thump in anticipation.

'I grew up in poverty. I know how awful it is.'

His tone was bleak. His eyes held hers for a moment, memories haunting him, punching her in the stomach.

He continued, 'I can't be responsible for putting my employees back into a situation where they are struggling on a daily basis to eat, to pay their bills. To see no future for themselves or their children. Having no choices in life. The shame and feelings of worthlessness.'

'You have strong memories of those days…of your childhood?'

'Yes.'

Things were starting to make sense now…his grandmother's kindness. 'Your grandmother taking me in…she feels responsible too?'

He nodded grimly. 'She's involved with a number of organisations for the homeless.'

Her heart tumbled to see the way he was trying to act detached, his stoic expression, the matter-of-fact way he spoke. When the tight lines at the corner of his eyes told another story.

'Were *you* homeless?'

He studied the rug for a few seconds, his arms folded in front of his chest. His head rose and he stared at her, with his jaw set in *don't pity me* tightness.

'For a few days, yes. My mother, grandmother and I had all moved from Puglia to Milan. We were staying with my mother's then boyfriend. They had a row. He threw us out. We had no money and nowhere to go.'

'How old were you?'

'Fourteen.'

What must it have been like to be a young teenage boy, facing living on the streets?

'Were you scared?'

'We slept for four nights in a doorway in a back alley. It was daunting…but the worst thing was the humiliation. I swore then that I would never allow it to happen again—that I would always protect my family from such embarrassment.'

'That's what drives you? The reason you put such pressure on yourself?'

'Yes.'

'But you need to accept what you have accomplished too, Matteo. Believe that if you did it once you can do it again. What's the point of everything you've achieved if you can get no happiness, no sense of reward from it?'

'That isn't of importance.'

'That you are happy? Satisfied? Why not?'

'If I'm satisfied I'll stop being so driven. And that's dangerous.'

'But you need both—to have drive and also to be happy.'

He shook his head vehemently, not prepared even to consider her arguments. 'I can't be complacent. Not in this industry.'

'Of course—I accept that. But maybe you need to accept what you've achieved—and most importantly believe that you *will* deal with whatever the future brings. Don't let the fear of poverty, of homelessness control you. They are only fears, thoughts… They're not a reality now. You've proved yourself, Matteo. By everything you have achieved. You need to believe that you can do the same again if necessary.'

His eyes narrowed, their coffee *gelato* now frozen rock-hard. 'Do *you* believe in yourself?'

She hated the way he had turned this back on her. But maybe, if she was honest with him, he might see that there was some merit in what she was saying.

'Probably not enough.'

She paused and realised that the burden of guilt she had been carrying around—about her parents, her accident, her wedding—felt a little lighter now that she had spoken about them and Matteo's insistence that she wasn't to blame.

'But you know what? Each time I've been knocked down I've come back... When my career in ballet was snapped away from me... My wedding. Other paths have opened up to me.'

He looked so burdened by the responsibilities he was carrying, she wanted to ease his tension, to see him smile again.

So with a cheeky grin she added, 'I even got to meet *you*—which has to be some consolation.'

The hard lines of his face dissolved into a charismatic smile—shining eyes and gorgeous white teeth. 'Whoa! Careful or I might get a big head.'

Trying not to swoon, she tried to adopt a cool-girl pose of easy nonchalance. 'Of all the men I have met, you are the one person who deserves to have a massive ego. But you don't.'

His head dipped. Was it her imagination or did

his cheeks colour ever so slightly? Crikey, this guy *really* knew how to get to a girl.

When he looked back up he cleared his throat, his expression telling her little of what he was thinking.

'I take nothing for granted.'

'Which is good...but maybe you should start enjoying what you have—even a little bit.'

He leaned towards her and those brown eyes were alight with mischief. 'I'm lying here on the floor with you when I have an important reception to host in less than two hours. Is that a good enough start for you?'

That expression about cutting off a limb in order to get something... Well, right now she understood it perfectly. Because every atom in her body was crying out to lean in towards him, to touch the smooth golden skin of his cheek, to touch her lips to his.

The friendship of a colleague.

She had to remember that was all she could—should—hope for.

With a man who set her alight with a single look.

A man who through his power, strength and empathy made her feel like a real-life Odette from *Swan Lake*.

CHAPTER SIX

EMMA STABBED THE 'send' button on her text message, clasped her phone tight in her fist and went and stood by her open bedroom door. She peeked down the frescoed corridor. It was empty. She stepped back into her room, quickly patting the loose curls of her pinned up hair, testing its stability.

Please, please let him read my message. And soon.

The first guests were due to arrive any moment now. She dashed across the room to the windows overlooking the Grand Canal.

A powerful motor boat was already approaching Ca' Divina's landing stage. The lights of other intimidatingly expensive boats were following in its wake.

She stepped a little closer to the window, the better to peer through the ripples of the antique glass. The scene below was illuminated by the discreet low lights on the landing stage. And just then the person waiting to disembark looked up at her.

Sebastian King! The world-famous composer.

She had seen his name on the guest list. But seeing him in reality was a whole different matter.

And now he was staring up at her, clearly amused.

She leapt away from the window. Her pounding heart was sending flames of heat onto her cheeks.

'Guests are already arriving. Why aren't you ready?'

She spun around, her heart slipping into a wild allegro beat.

Dressed in a dark midnight-blue suit, a light blue shirt and a navy and silver tie, Matteo did a pretty good job of filling the extrawide doorway.

She swung away from him and reached behind her to point a finger at the cause of her delay. 'I can't fasten the back of my dress. That's why I texted you. I need your help.'

She turned back in time to see his mouth tighten as he moved towards her and then she looked away. Back out to the lights shining from the delicately carved windows of the Gothic *palazzo* across the canal.

His scent wrapped around her. Musk with a hint of vanilla.

She dragged in a deep breath against the quiver in her belly.

He worked in silence, his fingers tracing against the top of her spine. She held herself rigid, determined not to let the threatening shivers escape.

But as his fingers moved across her bare skin she instinctively arched her back. Feeling totally exposed.

Her full-length gown had a wide cut-out section at the back, all the way down to her waist, exposing most of her spine. A gold chain was sewn into one border of the barely there side panels, and she needed Matteo to secure it to the gold clasp sewn onto the other side panel. With the gold chain unsecured she was in danger of the whole dress slipping off. Which, considering she was unable to wear a bra with this dress, was definitely not a good idea. Especially with a papal representative attending tonight.

'I expected you downstairs ten minutes ago.'

His voice, a sensual caress even when he was admonishing her, was so suggestive of carnal pleasures it left her rubber-boned.

She swallowed against the shimmers of desire skipping along her skin.

'The mixologist didn't arrive. I had to organise a replacement.'

Those strong hands twisted her around. A flicker of amusement sent golden sparkles radiating through his brown eyes.

'I like a martini with lemon peel.' Then the amusement in his eyes died and he inhaled a deep breath that spoke of hidden unease beneath his cool exterior. '*Andiamo*. Let's go.'

'I have to do my make-up.'

'You don't have time.'

He had to be kidding!

'I can't meet your guests with no make-up on.'

'Yes, you can.' His eyes travelled over her face, quietly devouring her. '*Sei bellissima.* You look beautiful.'

There was a low, seductive note to his voice and she suddenly felt light-headed.

'You don't need make-up. Your skin is perfect.'

His hand moved to take her elbow, and although her bones now felt like melting rubber she jumped out of his way and wobbled over to the dressing table. There she grabbed her favourite scarlet lipstick and quickly applied it, a swirling vortex of panic and desire spinning inside her as she tried to ignore Matteo's dark and dangerous reflection in the mirror glass.

She twisted back and ran to the stairs.

On the first step Matteo joined her and held his hand to her elbow, steadying her progress as she tottered down on much too high gold sandals that she would never have dared buy herself.

He pulled her to a stop halfway down and pointed at her feet unhappily. 'Those sandals are much too high for you. I asked for them to be delivered before I knew about your ankle.'

She took her arm from his continuing grip and placed her hand on his elbow instead. With a little push she urged him forward. 'They're fine, honestly. Let's go.'

She couldn't let him see how nervous she was about co-hosting the reception with him. How, now that it was an imminent reality, her self-confidence had fallen through the floor. She was a runaway bride, duped by her ex, rejected by her parents. A failed ballerina. How on earth was she supposed to entertain some of the world's highest achievers? She was about to let Matteo down. Let herself down.

They made it to the *portego* just as Sebastian King climbed the final steps of the stairs leading up from the landing stage.

Matteo and he embraced, with a lot of clapping each other on the back.

'Sebastian, let me introduce you to Emma Fox.'

Sebastian King was a big bear of a man, with a ruddy complexion, an easy smile and a tight crew cut that left only a light covering of grey stubble on his head. He took her hand, and then yanked her in for a hug.

'Was it you I saw staring out at me from the window?'

She gave him a non-committal smile and dared a quick look in Matteo's direction. He gave her a *what were you doing?* frown.

Time to move the conversation on.

'I'm so excited to meet you. I saw you perform

at The Lowry in Salford with my school. I was only twelve but I have such wonderful memories. I'm a huge fan.'

Sebastian gave a loud chuckle. 'Delighted to hear it, my dear. Been to see any of my recent work?'

She could feel herself pale. 'I'm afraid not. But I hope to.'

It was Sebastian's turn to look unimpressed. He twisted away. 'What direction is the bar?' His tone said that he needed a drink. *Now*. And some decent company.

She was about to apologise to Matteo for her less than auspicious start, but pulled back her words. Apologising would only add to her humiliation and her sense of not belonging here. Of being out of her depth. So instead she smiled warmly at a group of glittering guests coming towards them, her insides filling with dread.

She had nothing in common with any of these people. What was she going to say to them all? And what if something went wrong with the reception? Would she cope? Would Matteo forgive her?

The next half an hour passed in a whirl. She shook hands and smiled. Nodded as Matteo spoke to his guests, more often than not in rapid Italian, only understanding the occasional word. So much for the *Beginners' Italian* podcast she had listened to religiously every morning on the way to work, daydreaming of effortlessly ordering a *bellini* in Harry's Bar.

It had been arranged that the Chinese delegation would be the last guests to arrive—a silent signal of their importance and status. But as they began to ascend the stairs, stopping to point and gaze at the frescos and gilt-adorned walls and high ceilings, Matteo lowered his head and said in a low, urgent voice, 'Sadie and Johnny haven't arrived yet. I need to call her. Take the delegation through to the ballroom once I have greeted them. Introduce them to the other guests.'

Her stomach thumped to the floor. And her heart followed soon after. Apart from the famous faces, she wouldn't remember who was who.

She leaned closer to him, panic pumping through her body. Totally out of her depth. '*I'll* call Sadie. You go with Mr Xue and the rest of the delegation.'

He pulled back and gave her a curious look. 'But I have her private number—you don't. Is everything okay? You seem—'

She jumped in, not wanting to hear any more. She needed to pretend she was fine. She had asked for this job. She owed it to Matteo to deliver. 'Everything's fine. I just thought you would prefer to accompany Mr Xue into the ballroom, but I would be delighted to.'

He threw her another curious look. He obviously wasn't buying her breezy tone.

She led the delegation away and entered the ballroom with her heart doing a Viennese waltz. Her mind went blank when she was confronted by a sea of faces.

What did the President of the Region of Veneto and his wife look like again?

She needed to think. Get her act together. She was the one who'd promised Matteo that she was more than able for this role.

She called the translator to her side. 'Elena, I would like to introduce the group to the President of Veneto. Can you direct us towards him? And then will you please stay and translate? I will bring other guests over and introduce them to the delegation.'

For the next ten minutes she moved through the room with a coolness she definitely wasn't feeling, approaching other guests and inviting them to meet with the Chinese delegation. Each time she brought them forward she prayed she had got their names and titles right.

After what felt like several lifetimes of tight, terrified smiles and introductions, Emma gave a massive sigh of relief when she turned to find Matteo entering the room with Sadie Banks and Johnny North at his side. A shiver of recognition and excitement ran through the room.

Johnny North—her teenage crush.

Even more handsome and laid-back sexy in real life. Taller than she'd thought.

She stared at him, and second by second felt her teenage dreams fizzle away.

She gave a huff of disbelief.

Just like that her teenage crush had disappeared in a puff of smoke.

All thanks to Matteo.

He was her secret crush now.

A crush who was staring at her with a dark scowl.

She tried to wipe the starstruck expression off her face and gave him a quick, professional *I have everything under control* smile.

His shoulder twitched, but he turned away to speak to Sadie and then Johnny. Together they moved through the room. They spoke to the other guests with smiles and laughs as they walked but did not stop until they'd reached the Chinese delegation.

No longer needed, Emma slipped away to check on the rest of the *palazzo*. Glad to escape. Glad to be busy and to put a lid on how vulnerable she felt tonight.

First she checked in with the head of security. Then, in the lounge, she paused to watch the replacement mixologist tossing bottles of spirits and assorted fruit in the air, egged on by the crowd surrounding him, who were dancing to the beat of the music being played by the DJ in the corner.

Waiters were discreetly mingling amongst the guests with trays of Prosecco and the exquisite canapés she had tasted with the chef earlier, when she had given her approval for them to be served. Langoustine tails, gnocchi *fritti*, parmesan and poppyseed lollipops.

A magician dressed in eighteenth-century costume passed through the crowd performing tricks, adding to the carnival atmosphere.

Coming out from the lounge into the *portego*, she gave a brief smile to Matteo. He and Mr Xue were having their photo taken with Sadie and Johnny in front of a fresco showing Odysseus's ship in turbulent waters.

She walked away, but her spine tingled with the uncomfortable certainty that a set of unhappy, much too observant brown eyes were boring into her back.

She worked her way through the ballroom, checking that everything was going to plan. The string quartet were playing beautifully, at the perfect volume, the lighting was subtle, and the guests all had food and drink at hand.

Heading in the direction of the kitchen, to check in with the chef, she gave a small yelp when Matteo came up beside her and with a hand to her bare back silently guided her in the direction of his office.

Inside, he did not turn on the light.

He stepped close to her. 'Is everything okay?'

In the dark room he seemed even bigger than usual, his body acting like a magnet, drawing her in towards him against her will. She longed to place her hand on his waist, beneath his open jacket, against the cotton of his shirt, to feel the reassurance of his strength, of the tight muscles she had felt earlier when showing him the Pilates stretches.

She stepped away from him towards the faint outline of his desk. 'Yes, of course.'

'I want you to circulate amongst the guests and try to look like you are *enjoying* yourself.' He said the second half of the sentence in a tone of mild exasperation.

'I need to check that everything is running smoothly.'

'Yes, but as my co-host you need to relax… *Dio*, Emma, I don't want to have to worry about you tonight.'

Embarrassed heat licked against her skin. She gave silent praise that they were standing in the near dark. Her throat thick with disappointment that she was failing, she asked, in a much too high-pitched voice, 'What do you mean, worry about me?'

'You should be having fun—not looking as though this is hard work.'

'But it *is* work. I want to do it properly.' On the cusp of blurting out how overwhelmed she felt, she drew back from it and said in a self-mocking tone, 'I just don't know what to chat to the guests about… I can hardly speak to a Nobel Laureate about the weather, can I?'

'No, but you can enquire if he's enjoying Venice. Introduce him to some other guests. I need you to host alongside me.'

He spoke in a gentle voice, as if he was willing her to relax. To enjoy the night. He should be cross with her—angry, even. He didn't have the time to be taking her aside and encouraging her like a naïve intern.

Tears welled at the back of her eyes.

She swallowed hard. Pushed them away.

'Okay, I'll relax… It's just that I don't want to let you down tonight. I know how important this reception is to you.'

He stepped closer. He held her gaze.

'You're not letting me down.'

His voice was low, deep, sincere. Her heart did a *grand jeté* across her chest.

She opened her mouth to speak but no words came.

His hand moved up as though to touch her, but then dropped back to his side. 'I have to go.'

She nodded and he turned and left the room.

For a few minutes she leaned against the office wall, trying to compose herself.

Inhaling deep breaths.

Cracking her knuckles. That was something she hadn't done since she was a teenager. Hadn't done since the ballet master had rapped her on them for doing so.

Despite every logical warning her brain was yelling down to her heart, she had to face up to a certain fact: she was falling for Matteo. Physically…and perhaps emotionally. A psychologist would have a field day with her. No doubt the words 'rebound' and 'poor decision-making' would feature. These feelings were pointless. She did not *want* another relationship. Not that she supposed Matteo had any interest in her anyway, beyond physical attraction.

Her conversation with him earlier in the day came back to her…his insistence that she wasn't to blame for her past…his belief in her.

She pushed away from the wall. She had to stop her negative thoughts. Stop feeling so self-conscious and unsure. She was here to do a job.

She walked into the ballroom, full of great intentions. And straight into Johnny North. He gave her the smile that had stared back at her from her bedside locker throughout her boarding school years. That *come and rebel with me* smile. That had been her teenage desire. To rebel against the restrictions of boarding school, her parents' expectations.

A rush of excitement fizzed through her. It wasn't too late. She could still rebel, walk away from all her insecurities. Be tough and carefree. Forget the past and move with confidence into the future.

She held out her hand to him. 'Emma Fox.'

He shook her hand and asked in his American drawl, 'So, what brings you to Venice, Emma Fox?'

'I'm on the run.'

He gave her a grin of approval. 'You're my type of girl.'

Matteo tried to pay attention to the conversation between Mr Xue and Sebastian King about a concert Sebastian had conducted at the Beijing National Centre for the Performing Arts last year. But his attention was continually diverted across the room, to where Johnny North was holding court with a rapt audience of one. Emma. Pink-cheeked and dazzlingly radiant. Her porcelain skin glowing against the poppy-red colour of her dress.

Porcelain skin that was so soft it had sent juggernauts of lust powering through him earlier, when he had touched her bare back whilst fastening her dress.

He had longed to touch his lips against that skin…from the top of her long, elegant ballerina neck all the way down her spine.

Stopping to inhale her delicate rose scent.

Despite the saga of Sadie being late and needing to focus on the final subtle negotiations with Mr Xue, he had been seconds away from pulling her into his arms and kissing her soft mouth in the darkness and the seductive silence of his office.

Irritation twisted in his chest and he clenched his teeth. Okay, so she was mingling with the guests now, as he had asked, instead of dashing about the *palazzo*, clearly uncomfortable. But did she *have* to pick the most handsome guy in the room to chat to? And did she *have* to look so enthralled with him? And why wasn't she moving on? Talking to other guests? Talking to *him* instead of Johnny North.

He excused himself from his present company and made his way over to Emma and Johnny. Johnny had one shoulder touching against the frescoed wall of the ballroom. Matteo gave him a lethal stare and without batting an eyelid Johnny moved away from the wall. Matteo stood next to Emma and placed a hand on her lower back. Sometimes men didn't need any words.

Nearby, Sadie left the company of a group of national politicians, cross-party differences forgotten in their collective star-struck veneration as Sadie flashed them her trademark traffic-stopping smile, and swept towards them to plant a kiss on Johnny's cheek. He pulled her tighter towards him and whispered something into her ear. Sadie giggled and gave him a playful push.

As one they looked up, love and happiness radiating from their every pore.

Beside him, Emma tensed.

Sadie moved forward and extended her hand. 'Hi, I'm Sadie… Sadie North.' She laughed and gestured helplessly. 'I'm still getting used to saying my married name.'

Emma smiled, but lines of tension pulled at the corners of her eyes.

'Are you from Venice, Emma, or are you visiting too?'

'She's running away, apparently,' Johnny said, with a wink in Emma's direction.

Sadie clapped her hands in delight. 'Really? How exciting! I couldn't think of anywhere more awesome to run to. Right? Isn't Venice seriously incredible? Gosh, so many times in the past I was tempted to run away. Especially from some of the directors I have had to work with! Not to mention some of the disastrous relationships I've had.'

Sadie paused and, looking in Matteo's direction, gave a light laugh.

'Not counting *you*, Matteo, you were one of the good ones.'

Beside him he could feel Emma stiffen even more. Sadie had no filter. Maybe that was what made her such an acclaimed actor. She was open and candid and most of the time she got away with it, because people found her directness and fun personality refreshing. But tonight, on the high of new love, she was oblivious to the signals Emma was giving that this conversation was making her uncomfortable.

But perhaps it was just he who could read Emma? Maybe others wouldn't see the subtle signals. It was a thought way too disturbing to spend time pondering on.

Sadie's hand moved onto Johnny's chest. 'But now I no longer want to run.'

The honeymooning couple shared an intense and private look.

Emma flinched.

His stomach dipped with sharp regret.

For Emma. For himself.

What Sadie and Johnny shared they would never have.

Sadie twisted back to them, her eyes shining with the wonder only those newly in love and small children could conjure. 'Isn't Venice so cool? The buildings, the food, the canals, the Carnival…it's all so beautiful. It's just perfect for a honeymoon.' She turned to Johnny, who was looking down at her with fond amusement.

'I want to come back here for each of our anniversaries.'

Emma's body gave up a hard tremor that vibrated against his hand. She was staring at Sadie and Johnny with a haunted expression. Shame and guilt ripped through him.

He needed to get her away from here. He should have anticipated this.

But before he could speak Sadie said, 'Matteo, you never told me about Emma. How long have you been together?'

He forced himself to give a casual shrug. 'We're just colleagues.'

'Ah. That's a shame. You're cute together.'

He gave a tight smile. 'We had better circulate.'

Then, to his horror, he realised that there were tears in Emma's eyes.

He was about to suggest that they step out onto the terrace for a moment when Elena the interpreter approached.

'I'm sorry to interrupt, Signor Vieri, but Mr Xue has asked to meet with you in private.'

It could only mean one thing. Mr Xue was ready to sign the contracts. His instinct that the deal would be finalised on the news that Sadie and Johnny would open the collection had been right.

He should get those contracts signed now. He had copies ready and waiting in his office.

But what about Emma? Could he leave her in this vulnerable state?

Should he talk to her, reassure her, and let Mr Xue wait?

It should be no contest.

His business, or this woman he had only known for a matter of days.

He leaned down towards Emma and said, 'I'll be back in a little while.'

He gave a swift nod to Sadie and Johnny before walking towards Mr Xue, Elena following.

Alone with Sadie and Johnny, Emma looked at the honeymooning couple, who were now playfully teasing each other, oblivious to her. Oblivious to the entire room.

For the first time since the police had knocked at her door in the middle of the night she felt her heart shatter. The shock and disbelief were finally giving way to the reality of everything she had lost. All those fantasies she'd had of a beautiful wedding day. A romantic honeymoon. Of finding her own family.

Her heart shattered because she and her ex had never had the love, the fun, the chemistry that was between Sadie and Johnny.

Her heart shattered out of happiness for the couple before her. Touched by the magic playing between them. Touched by the glow lighting up their eyes. Touched by the heartbreaking happiness pulsating from them both.

Her heart shattered because Matteo hadn't realised just how hard it was for her to witness a couple on honeymoon, to hear Sadie talk so exuberantly about her time in Venice.

Or maybe he had realised and had still opted to go and speak to Mr Xue.

And who could blame him with so much at stake?

He'd made the right decision.

But that didn't stop the hurt. Didn't stop the loneliness creeping along her veins. The reality that she was alone in this world. The horrible hollowness in her soul.

We're just colleagues.

His words to Sadie gathered around her shattered heart like barbed wire.

She shouldn't want anything else but the friendship of a colleague. But the chemistry between them was so intense, so personal, it was hard to keep it at bay.

And now everything was mixed up. People thought she was here as Matteo's partner. Nobody had realised she was the event co-ordinator. Had she compromised her professional standing?

She distractedly said goodbye in Sadie and Johnny's direction, but they were so taken up in each other she wasn't sure if they even noticed her walk away.

She moved about the *palazzo*, trying to focus on managing the reception. She forced herself to stop and talk briefly to some of the guests, but she felt too vulnerable. Too confused.

Was her attraction to Matteo just a way of not facing the pain of her wedding imploding? A distraction from guilt and sadness and her fears for the future? Was she hoping he'd save her instead of saving herself?

Back inside the ballroom, the quartet had been replaced by a jazz band with a soulful lead singer who reminded Emma of Ella Fitzgerald. Couples were out on the dance floor, dancing to a slow number.

'*Vuoi ballare?* Do you want to dance?'

She arched her neck away, a long shiver of awareness darting down her spine at Matteo's question, breathed against her ear from behind... a slow, sensual caress on her exposed neck.

He didn't wait for her to answer. Instead he took her hand and led her out onto the dance floor.

He held her close to him and they moved to the slow rhythm of the music.

She tried to resist him, her body rigid as she stared at the fine navy wool of his jacket.

He pulled her closer, whispered in a teasing, sexy tone, 'Relax, I don't bite...unless provoked.'

Immediately she felt undone.

His hand resting on her hip sent waves of desire to the centre of her body. She yearned for his thumb to stroke the delicate skin around her hip bone.

Standing so close to him, surrounded by his raw potency, one hand resting on his broad shoulder, her other hand lost in his grasp, she felt her heart double over, craving intimacy and closeness with him.

She stared at the broad silver and navy diagonal lines of his tie. Wanting to move even closer to him. Knowing she should move away. Protect herself. Be nothing more than his employee. Be a strong and independent woman who thought of nothing but her career. Who didn't fall for false fantasies.

She dared a quick glance up into those golden-brown eyes which stared back at her with open concern.

That concern could either undo her or reinforce her resolve to be distant from him. She chose the latter. 'I thought you had a meeting with Mr Xue?'

'I've organised for us to meet tomorrow morning instead.'

Confused, she asked, 'I assumed he wanted to meet about signing the contracts—are they still holding out?'

'No, just now Mr Xue confirmed that he wants

to sign. There are some small outstanding issues that still need to be resolved, but they won't be a problem. I decided that we should wait until tomorrow to address those.'

Why hadn't he wanted to sign tonight? She knew how important those contracts were to him. A horrible thought occurred to her.

'Were you worried about leaving the party…? If you'd had another co-host would you have taken the time to sign the contracts tonight?'

He held her gaze, his expression sombre. 'I should have realised meeting Sadie and Johnny would be difficult for you.'

'No… Yes… But that was no reason to put off the signing.'

'It can wait.'

'But why, when it's so important to you?'

His mouth thinned. 'You're an employee and I put you in a difficult situation. I take the welfare of all my employees seriously. I could see that you needed my support.'

This wasn't what she wanted. She didn't want to need him. Or anyone else. She wanted, *needed* to stand on her own two feet. To be independent.

'I can manage by myself. I don't need you.'

Those brown eyes held hers with an assured certainty. His mouth was a serious line.

'Yes, you do.'

CHAPTER SEVEN

STANDING BESIDE MATTEO on Ca' Divina's landing stage, Emma waved goodbye to the last of the guests before curling her arms tight against her waist. Warming herself. Fending off the pinpricks of awareness that she was alone once again with Matteo. Not quite certain how she felt about that.

It was gone one in the morning. Most of the other guests had left two hours ago. But the remaining group—associates of Matteo—had stayed and chatted around the outside terrace table, wrapped up in coats and blankets, warmed by outside heaters and *grappa*, snug against the cold February air, while the staff had tidied up inside.

Matteo had insisted that everyone speak in English, so that Emma was included in the conversation. He had kept her by his side all evening, his hand resting on her back, guiding her as they moved amongst the guests. It was a hand that was way too comforting. A hand that had at times fooled her into feeling that she had found someone who would care for her; protect her—

before her brain kicked in and told her that she was a fool.

It was all nothing more than a rebound fantasy. She was projecting onto Matteo her need for security. Her fears for the future. All the uncertainties facing her. Where would she live? How long before she got a job? Before her meagre savings ran out?

And that wasn't fair on him. Or herself.

He was her boss—a colleague.

Nothing else.

He didn't want a relationship.

The lights and the noise of the engine on the launch taking the guests away faded across the water. The only sound that remained was the lap of water against the walls of the *palazzo* and the landing stage.

'I'm sorry about Sadie; I should have realised that meeting someone on honeymoon would be upsetting for you.'

He spoke slowly, as though needing her to understand the sincerity of his words.

She bunched her hands in the pockets of her wool coat, felt the soft material grating against the tension in her fists. She needed to keep this conversation professional. Keep her guard up against his employer's concern. Against how physically aware she was of him.

'I didn't need you to cancel the meeting with Mr Xue.'

He pointed towards the *palazzo*, gesturing for them to head back inside. 'You were upset. I couldn't leave you…especially when I could have prevented it.'

The red carpet, hastily organised via a business contact of the caterers, still remained on the wooden landing stage, soaking up the sound of their footsteps.

'But why delay signing the contract?'

Matteo held open one of the heavy wood-panelled double front doors for her, and then busied himself shutting and securing it once they were both inside. When finished he turned and regarded her with a look she couldn't quite decipher.

The hired staff had left prior to the departure of the last of the guests. Matteo now locking the two of them into the *palazzo*, all alone, suddenly felt very intimate. Very personal.

He took off his coat, dipping his head down. When he looked up his jaw worked for a few seconds, as if he were fighting something inside himself.

'You said today that I need to believe I can deal with whatever life throws at me. You're right.'

He paused for a short breath, but then continued on at a fast pace. Sounding as though he needed to say all this now or never.

'I need to stop worrying about the future; it's too draining. For as long as I can remember I've felt a huge burden of responsibility. It's still there, but I need to get things into perspective and know what my priorities should be.'

'You didn't need to delay the meeting because of me...or insist I stay with you all night. I'm an employee...I don't expect any of that from you.'

Her voice echoed off the high ceilings of the entrance hall. Sharp and petulant.

He walked to the stairs and waited on the bottom step for her to follow. A new tension pulled on his mouth. When she'd joined him he pointed down at her sandals.

'Take them off.'

Taken aback, she stared down at her feet blankly. And then, not quite knowing why, she set her mouth into a fierce scowl. 'No.'

He glared at her, his eyes dark with anger... and passion.

A current of desire whooshed through the air.

He flung his coat onto the balustrade. It slid for a second before coming to a stop beside one of the carved figures of a young woman holding a light aloft that topped both of the stairs' newel posts.

He placed his hands on his hips.

She gave him a *don't you dare* stare.

Which only seemed to embolden him.

In one quick movement he was beside her. Then he was walking up the stairs with her in his arms.

She wanted to demand to know what he thought he was playing at. But she wouldn't give him the satisfaction of showing she cared enough to ask.

Crushed against the hard heat of his chest, the muscles of his forearm tense beneath her back, she felt long fingers clasp around her outer thigh. She refused to look up at him. Flames of desire burned in her belly.

He dropped her at the top of the stairs and gave her a stare of utter exasperation. 'I could see that you needed support tonight. Why are you blaming me for wanting to be there for you?'

Her confusion boiled and simmered inside her, along with frustration. Because she damn well wanted him to kiss her right now. To feel his body pushed against hers.

'You're my boss!'

He threw his hands upwards at her shouted words, but something in his eyes—a tiny hesitation before he spoke—told her that he too had his doubts about what was happening between them.

'So? Can't a boss care?'

No. Not when there's fire between you.

She rubbed her hand against the tightness in her temple 'It's all getting too confusing.'

He didn't speak, and in the unsettling silence

she pretended a sudden fascination with Odysseus's ship on the wall behind his shoulder.

'I'm fond of you, Emma. I want to help.'

His low-spoken words curled around her. Like a tight fist around her heart.

She wanted to tell him that she was afraid. Afraid of falling for him. Afraid of how intensely she liked him already. Afraid of how attracted she was to him.

With a helpless questioning show of her palms, she gave him a truth she could hide behind. 'Why help...when I'm more of a burden to you than anything else?'

'No.'

He moved closer. His eyes dared her to look away, to deny what he was saying.

'I like spending time with you. I like how you stand up to me. Your sense of humour. Your enthusiasm.'

She couldn't listen to this. She had to ignore his words and how badly her heart wanted to believe him.

She shook her head and gave him a teasing frown. Pretended that it was all rather amusing. 'Really? I spend more time in tears than anything else.'

'You found out on your wedding day that the man you were about to marry was corrupt—of *course* you're in tears.'

Hearing his blunt words killed the pretence. And in the face of his soft, searching eyes which refused to look away, the truth bubbled out of her.

'I don't know what I want any longer.'

Embarrassed by her admission, she moved away and walked over to the window overlooking the canal on the opposite side of the room.

So much for being tough.

How did Matteo manage to get to her every time they spoke?

How did he manage to cut through every pretence?

Why did she feel protected yet in deep danger whenever she was with him?

When Matteo eventually joined her they both stared out of the floor-to-ceiling picture window to the lights of Venice. In a low, matter-of-fact voice, he said, 'I have to leave on Sunday for New York Fashion Week. We have two more days together.'

His eyes swept over her face, waiting for a response. She looked at him blankly, feeling numb at his words. Two days. That was all.

His chest rose heavily as he inhaled a deep breath. 'Mr Xue and his team are travelling to Verona tomorrow after our early-morning meeting. I would like to spend the rest of the day with you—show you Venice.' His mouth curled downwards and he shrugged. 'But it's up to you.'

She needed to understand why he was being so kind to her. What did he want? What could she possibly give him?

'Why are you doing this?'

His eyes narrowed, impatience flaring. 'Why did you spend time showing me those Pilates moves today?'

She didn't have to think about her answer.

'Because I wanted to help you.'

But she stopped herself before she could add, *And I wanted to spend time with you, connect with you. Touch you.*

A reluctant smile grew on his mouth. But his eyes stayed startlingly sober. 'Just as I want to help *you.*'

She closed her eyes for a moment. What was she going to do?

She was still unsure when she opened them again. But seeing him silhouetted against the backdrop of Venice, his face set hard with pride, his eyes burning bright with the strength of his commanding but compassionate personality, she knew he would only ask once. If she said no, the next two days would be nothing more than a business formality.

'I would like to see Venice with you.'

She had tried to speak in a dispassionate voice, but it came out in a rushed whisper.

He nodded, not giving any other reaction, and

she spun away, gabbling, 'I'll see you in the morning…'

She was almost at the stairs when he called out, 'You'll need help undoing your dress.'

Her heart and stomach collided midway in her body, and then sickeningly ricocheted back to where they belonged.

She rolled her shoulders before walking towards him, telling herself just to get it over and done with. He was a colleague. Undoing her dress. Nothing more.

She slipped off her coat and turned her back to him.

His hand touched against her skin.

She jerked away.

Desire—strong, excruciating, wonderful—streamed through her, pooling in her core. Exquisite pressure.

He made no comment, but stepped closer.

His fingertips grazed her skin again. She dipped her head against the fresh wave of need which engulfed her, leaving her afraid to breathe.

The unclasped chain fell downwards, its heavy cool weight swinging like a pendulum against her bare skin.

She should move away. But she stood there and wrapped her hands around her waist. Vulnerable. Exposed. Electrified.

His hand touched the top of her spine. And

then, inch by inch, ran down her back to her waist. A definite, deliberate movement. The movement of a man wanting to possess.

Her body gave another intense shiver.

His lips briefly skimmed the top of her shoulder blade.

For a moment she stood there, hoping he would go further. But then she understood. There would be nothing more. Tonight.

She walked away from him, each step an effort. Walked away from the one place where she belonged.

The following morning Matteo left the Hotel Cipriani with a burning sense of having been robbed.

The Chinese deal had been signed.

He felt relieved. But nothing else.

None of the sense of accomplishment that usually came with such a major deal. None of the pleasure that he'd taken yet another step up on the ladder of life, away from the lower rungs that led to the crypts of poverty.

He should be happier.

He manoeuvred his boat around the busy traffic on the Grand Canal, irritation and tiredness destroying any hope of him revelling in his success in the beauty of the Old Lady of the Lagoon on a blue-sky spring morning.

He had woken early, doubts whispering in his ear.

What had he done? Why the hell hadn't he signed the deal last night, when Mr Xue had been ready to do so? What if Mr Xue had changed his mind overnight? Just what had he sacrificed for a woman he'd only known for a handful of days?

Last night at the reception it had felt so right to want to be with her. To want to protect her. To actually *do* something about her resonating words earlier, telling him that he must believe, trust that he could handle whatever life threw at him. That he couldn't allow his fear of poverty, of failing others, to control him.

But in the darkness none of that had seemed so obvious, so right.

He couldn't go back to Ca' Divina yet. Even though he wanted to see her. Wanted to hear her voice. Wanted the calm that formed in his stomach every time he was with her.

The unfathomable sense of belonging that settled on his heart when he was with her.

He needed to clear his head.

At Ca' Foscari he swung the boat towards Campo Santa Margherita in the *sestiere* of Dorsoduro.

As ever, the picturesque square was a serene refuge. Locals were enjoying an early coffee at the cafés lining the square, buying bread at the bakery reputed to be the best in Venice, others were buying fish and vegetables at the market stalls.

Usually he would order an espresso at the bar and drink it quickly. Always pressed for time. Today he sat out at one of the pavement tables with his espresso.

Dog walkers, grandparents holding the hands of unsteady toddlers, students from the local university—all ambled through the square. Happy to enjoy the start of another Carnival day.

When had he last sat and watched others go by?

Had he ever?

Emma.

She was changing everything.

With her he felt a connection, a bond that was familiar, comforting, yet exhilarating. A physical attraction that was tearing him apart. But there was also her intelligence, her sense of fun. Her vulnerability.

Her pride, her resilience, her strength.

She had lost her career, her family, and had battled to rebuild her life. And now she was determined to rebuild it once again, in the face of yet another abysmal setback.

Yesterday, when she had shown him the Pilates moves, she had done so with such serious intent that he'd known it was important to her to see him better. She cared for him. He could see it in her eyes. In the way her body rocked towards him.

He drained his cup and stared up at the fifteenth-century carving set high up in the building. Santa Margherita and the dragon who had tried to consume her.

His heart suddenly lurched and began to free-fall.

His mind buzzed.

He fought the realisation forming there. Tried to put a stake in the heart of that thought. But it fought back. Ready to consume him.

He was falling in love with Emma.

Was that possible?

The dragon was open-mouthed. Ready to attack again.

This wasn't what he wanted.

This was his worst nightmare.

To fall in love.

He had seen how love had destroyed his mother. Had destroyed his childhood.

This was the last thing he'd ever wanted.

To fall in love with a woman who couldn't, *wouldn't* love him back.

How many times had she said she didn't want to be in love?

She reminded him of himself. Of how definite he'd been about not wanting love.

Until she'd came along.

He was falling in love with the one woman he couldn't have.

This couldn't be happening.

This was why he had always sworn he would never love.

He had stopped believing in love when he was a teenager. Knowing that ultimately it would destroy you.

He felt sick.

He had to pull back.

He had to detach himself from her.

But he couldn't walk away. Not yet.

He wanted the next few days. He wanted to be with her.

Two days. No more.

The scheming crocodile loitered behind the little boy who was happily fishing, oblivious to the danger he was in. The children standing in a corner of Campo San Polo, enraptured by the puppet show, shouted and screamed for the little boy to run away.

Their shouts were deafening, and Emma playfully grimaced in the direction of Matteo. But he didn't notice her. In fact for the past half an hour, since they had left Ca' Divina, he had been distant. Distracted.

A vine of anxiety wrapped itself around her left ankle—not quite hurting, but tight enough to warn her what was to come if she didn't shake off her uneasiness.

What was the matter?

Was he already regretting his decision to spend the day with her?

The sun slanted off his face, highlighting his golden skin. His thick dark eyelashes only occasionally flickered, as though he was in a trance. His mouth was a constant thin line.

Nervous attraction zinged through her veins. She clenched her hand against the temptation to reach out. To touch his cheek. To whisper, *Is everything okay?* To have him smile again.

This morning she had lain in bed, her body twisted towards the bedroom window and the majestic pale pastel buildings and faded red-tiled rooftops beyond. Knowing she had two choices.

Give in to her fear that she would be hurt and walk away now. Away from this too intense, too soon, too confusing relationship.

Or embrace these two remaining days. Two days that could give her a lifetime of happy memories.

But for that to happen she *had* to remember their relationship was boss and employee—colleagues at best. Nothing more.

She moved closer to him and rested her hand on his arm. He looked down at her with a frown, as if he was unsure of everything about her. For a moment awkwardness, suspicion, doubt passed between them.

The twisting sack in her chest tightened. He had changed his mind.

His eyes held hers but then flew away. As if he didn't want to look there.

She was about to make a joke—anything to lighten the tension between them—when she stopped herself. She was doing it again. Being passive. Afraid to rock the boat. Afraid that Matteo might reject her. Afraid that if she spoke her mind he might be angry, dismissive, provoked. Everything she had spent her childhood trying to prevent.

Her stomach lurched and her throat suddenly felt like nothing more than a thin straw through which she had to speak.

It would be so much easier to smile. To jolly him along. Not to have to face the reason why he now didn't want to be here with her.

The spacious square reverberated to the sound of voices. Friends chatting loudly outside pavement cafés. Children chasing around the fountain. Others giggling and whooping on the temporary ice rink. The sounds echoed off the surrounding tall historic buildings.

Sounds which made the silence between them as they walked through the square even more pronounced.

She cleared her throat. 'We can go home if

you like.' Her trepidation was hidden behind her sharp, snappy, defensive tone.

He looked at her impassively, as if quietly contemplating her offer. No quick denial, as she had secretly hoped.

'Do you want to?'

No! He wasn't turning this back on her.

She was about to tell him so when her phone began to ring. She flung open her handbag, leaving the two handles hanging from her forearm, and began to rummage through it. Where was it? She could hear it, but for the life of her she couldn't find it.

With a huff, she moved to the window of a nearby antique shop, dominated by the huge gilt frame of a dark religious artwork, and balanced her bag on the stone window ledge as she continued her search. Eventually she found it—under a pile of paperwork.

It was the tour guide, calling from Verona to give her an update on how the Chinese delegation was faring.

She spoke to the guide with her back deliberately towards Matteo, but in the window's reflection she could see that he was staring at her, his arms folded impatiently.

Dressed in a grey wool overcoat, open at the collar to reveal a light blue shirt and a navy pullover, his broad frame loomed large in the window reflection. Dark and menacing. And unfairly gorgeous.

Her anger, her defensiveness, was sinking as fast as it had risen.

When she turned back to him she had reverted to her professional mode. 'That was the tour guide. The group have booked in to their hotel and are about to tour the city. I've confirmed that they need to be back in Venice at five tomorrow, as the ball is starting at eight.'

Tomorrow evening Matteo was hosting the delegation at one of the Carnival's masked balls. She would be Matteo's partner again.

It would be their last event together.

The morning after he would be leaving for New York.

They might never see each other again.

That thought had her inhaling a deep breath against the loneliness that sideswiped her.

The vine clinging to her ankle tightened.

She opened her handbag and threw her phone back into its depths.

Matteo stared in after it. 'I'm surprised that you were able to find your phone in the first place...' He paused and grimaced, as if he was looking into the bowels of hell. 'In *there*.'

Did he have to sound so appalled?

'A woman's handbag is her business. Nobody else's.'

He tucked his arms into a tighter fold across his chest. And shot her an unimpressed eyebrow-raise.

She was about to ignore him. But then the new Emma stepped forward. The Emma who had got on the plane at Heathrow, determined to have her week in Venice. The Emma who'd sworn she would be tough and take no nonsense from anyone again.

Well, she was going straight to the top in giving someone a piece of her mind: Matteo Vieri, the Italian god of fashion.

Her jaw jutted out.

Her shoulder blades were so rigid she reckoned they would easily slice someone in two.

'I had a childhood of not being able to have a hair out of place, in a sterile home that smelt of bleach. That's to blame for my preference for messiness. What about you…? What's made *you* so proper…so strait-laced?'

So the legendary Matteo Vieri *could* do astonishment.

His mouth dropped open for a couple of seconds. And then it slammed shut.

His hands landed on his hips 'Strait-laced?'

'Yes…nothing is ever out of place in Ca' Divina. You are always immaculately groomed. Cufflinks always perfectly aligned, your hair always looking like you're on a fashion shoot. Do you *ever* look messy?'

His expression shifted from narked to nonchalant, as did his tone. 'I own several luxury goods companies. It's my duty to look good. I'm representing my businesses.'

True. But that didn't mean he didn't have down time. Time when he relaxed.

'Do you even *own* a pair of jeans? A tee shirt?'

He gestured to a street that ran beside the church of San Polo, indicating that they start walking again.

The street quickly narrowed to a laneway that could barely accommodate them both walking side by side. She tucked her handbag closer. Worried that in the tight confines she would bump into him. Worried that she might not be able to move away if she did.

'I own…a pair of jeans.'

His deadpan voice held a poorly disguised hint of humour.

A smile broke on her mouth. 'One! Most men I know own at least a dozen.'

His mouth twisted but his eyes were alight with humour. 'Well, I'm *not* most men, am I?'

Despite the shadows of the narrow alleyway, the day suddenly felt bright. Hopeful.

She gave him a cheeky smile. 'No. You're certainly not.'

He smiled back. The doubts, the unease of earlier erased.

They crossed over a canal and he led her down another side alleyway. 'We need to buy you a mask for the ball tomorrow night. There's an atelier down here, close to Campo San Rocco.'

Along the alleyway they passed two boys kicking a soccer ball against a wall, the dull thud in competition with their lively lyrical chatter.

'I liked your friends last night.'

Mischief sparked in his eyes. 'You sound surprised.'

Her mouth twitched. She cleared her throat. 'They're different to you—more laid-back.'

He slowed down as they approached a shop window adorned with masks. Some were stark and frightening, with long, exaggerated pointed noses—the masks of death and plague. Others were ornate and elegant, wisps of beauty and intrigue.

He caught her teasing tone and threw it back to her with an amused shrug. 'I guess…'

He rolled his shoulders and his eyes grew serious.

'Last night I remembered what you said yesterday about trying to enjoy life more, not worrying about the future.' He gave her a small smile. 'I think you might be right, so I've decided I want to spend time with my friends. In the past I wouldn't have asked them to stay, wanting to catch up with work instead.' He paused and a brief storm of doubt passed over his expression. Quickly it cleared to calm certainty. 'I also wanted them to meet you.'

Not even trying to pretend that she wasn't shocked by what he'd said, she asked, 'Why?'

'You mean a lot to me.'

What did he mean by that?

She opened her mouth to ask, but clamped it shut again.

She didn't want to hear his answer.

She wasn't ready for any of this.

So she laughed and said, 'You could have fooled me! All morning you've been acting as though you don't want to be here.'

For a moment he looked as if he was going to argue. His eyes swept over her. Her heart pleaded with him not to. Something even deeper within her pleaded with him to tell her that he felt what she did too.

He tugged at the bottom of his coat sleeves, a rueful grin transforming his expression to one of playful teasing. 'I didn't get enough sleep last night, and I woke early. Can we start again?'

'Do I hear the hint of an apology in there?'

'Yes. I'm sorry.' His smile grew even wider, a sexy challenge now sparkling in his eyes. 'Now, I think it's about time you and I had a little fun.'

CHAPTER EIGHT

AN HOUR LATER, close to Campo San Giacomo dell'Orio, in the *sestiere* of Santa Croce, they paused for lunch at one of Matteo's favourite restaurants in Venice—Alloro. The tiny restaurant, located on the banks of a narrow canal, had a dark wooden interior infused with over a century's worth of cooking aromas: garlic and rosemary, the earthiness of truffle, the hit-you-at-the-back-of-the-throat power of Asiago d'Allevo cheese.

Emma, bright-cheeked from the sharp February air, handed the blue and purple striped box containing her mask for tomorrow night's ball and her navy woollen coat to the maître d', who then showed them to their table overlooking the canal.

Their knees clashed as they settled into the small table, and for a few brief seconds a blast of heat fired between them. Deep longing. Two souls in need.

Emma was the first to look away. Her hands moved quickly to tuck a loose curl behind her ear before she straightened first her knife and then her fork on the starched white linen tablecloth.

He poured them both some water, his gut twisting.

So much for staying detached, unaffected by the realisation that he was falling for her. He had spent most of the morning quarrelsome and argumentative, frustrated with every feeling he had for her.

But the truth of his attraction to her had been determined to leak out. His willpower had proved useless against the continual adrenaline rush of physical chemistry and the emotional connection of being with her. Hope and pleasure were strongarming fear and resistance.

In the designer's studio she had tried on various styles of masks, at first carefully watching for his reaction.

But then something dark and sensual had whipped between them.

Her eyes had toyed with him from behind the masks. Dancing hazel eyes that could be his undoing.

They had grown bolder and bolder in their teasing and flirting.

Casual touches had skittered across his skin, jolts of pure pleasure.

Smiles had spoken of heart-pounding delicious desire.

For the first time ever he wasn't listening to his own cool logic. The logic that was telling him to walk away. That this was uncharted territory he shouldn't be meddling in. That to have had his heart broken as a child was one thing. To have it broken as an adult would be a whole different matter.

Opposite him, Emma stared at the lunch menu with a frown, her lips silently shaping the words she was reading.

'Would you like some help deciding?'

She shook her head without looking up, her expression fierce. 'No, thank you.'

He smiled to himself. Another piece of his heart was falling for this determined woman.

The waiter returned with a glass of Prosecco for Emma and white wine for him, as he had ordered.

On a deep breath Emma placed her food order in faltering Italian.

The waiter advised her, also in Italian, that her risotto would take thirty minutes to prepare. She blushed and looked at the waiter clearly confused.

Matteo translated for her, trying not to smile.

She nodded that it was okay, giving the waiter a faint smile.

When the waiter left, he lifted his glass. 'To new friends.'

Emma touched her glass to his and then gave

a quick shoulder-roll. She drew in a deep breath. *'Ai nuovi amici.'*

'I'm impressed.'

'No, my pronunciation is terrible. I tried to learn some Italian before the wed—'

Her eyes swept away from his.

At first she grimaced. Then a haunting sadness settled over her features. Remembering the past was physically hurting her.

He shifted in his seat, his heels digging into the parquet floor.

Top notes of disgust and anger filled his nostrils to think of her ex, but deep in his belly the only note was one of jealousy.

She had almost married another man.

What if he had seen her out on the streets of Venice with her new husband?

Would the rage of attractión he had felt for her the first time they'd met still have been the same even though she was in the arms of another man?

Would he have walked away with a sense of loss?

With feelings he couldn't process for a woman he had merely passed in the street?

But would he have been better off if he *had* only seen her from a distance?

Would he have been better off never even setting eyes on her?

He lanced those uncomfortable, troubling

thoughts with a question that drew him back to the reality of their situation.

'What are your plans for the future?'

Emma tugged at the neck of her cream polo-neck jumper. The same jumper she had worn the first night they had met.

'I'm going back to London.'

'To your old job?'

Her hand rubbed against her neck and then patted upwards to the base of her ponytail, her fingers attempting to smooth down the renegade curls that insisted on breaking free from the confines of her elastic band.

'No. I want to start afresh. I've enjoyed this week, so I've decided that I want to work in event management full-time.'

'You've done an excellent job for me. I'm sure you'll be very successful.'

She rested an arm on the table, a shoulder and an eyebrow rising simultaneously in challenge. 'I wouldn't go so far as saying *excellent*.'

'You're intelligent, flexible, personable and warm…and most of the time you're organised. You have all the traits needed to be a successful event manager.'

A deep blush erupted from the depths of her jumper, spewing upwards. She angled herself away from him, a hand hiding the lower half of her face. Pride and embarrassment vied for dominance in her gaze.

Ultimately neither won. Instead she batted away his words with a smile that was too fleeting, too nervous, too forced.

'And what's in the future for Matteo Vieri? World domination?'

She didn't trust him.

She didn't trust what he said.

He gritted his teeth and tried to ignore the sharp tap of her distrust that was prodding against his heart like the tip of a sword.

Threatening to stab him.

He slowly twisted the circular base of his wine glass on the linen cloth. Disquiet rolled in his stomach. *He needed to protect himself.*

'It's going to be a busy year. I have all the upcoming Fashion Weeks, I'm looking to expand aggressively into South America and I'm in the midst of a major renovation of my villa on Lake Garda.'

She nodded. And nodded again.

She yanked once more at the neck of her jumper. Beneath it her throat worked. Her pale toffee-mixed-with-peppermint eyes held his, but with a hesitancy, a sadness that sent that emotional sword she wielded straight through his raging heart.

'We're both going to be busy.'

Yes. Living separate lives.

The waiter arrived with their antipasti: asparagus and quail eggs for Emma, *carpaccio* for him.

He lifted his knife and fork, tasted his food and lowered his cutlery again.

Too distracted to eat.

The urge to connect with her, to reach out, detonated within him.

Without any thought he heard himself blurt out, 'When I was a child I lived close to here for a few years.'

Why had he told her that?

She too lowered her cutlery, her antipasto barely touched. 'What do you remember?'

Tension pinged like electric shocks in the small of his back. He moved forward in his chair and rested both arms on the table, stretching his spine. 'The apartment was on the third floor. I could see the Frari Campanile clearly from my bedroom window. At night, I used to pretend that...'

The words that had been spilling out of him dried up in an instant.

He had never spoken to anyone about his childhood before now.

He needed to stop.

'Pretend what?'

He didn't answer her question. Instead he stared down at the brilliant whiteness of the tablecloth, the loneliness of those years engulfing him.

Itchy, suffocating heat blasted his insides.

Her knees bumped against his. Her hands landed on his.

Long, slim, pale hands that sat lightly against his skin.

Not cloying or overpowering.

Just there.

His heart decelerated.

He closed his eyes.

Eventually he spoke. Needing to tell her. 'I used to pretend that my father watched me from the Frari Campanile. That he had come...that he had found me.'

'Found you...what do you mean?'

Her voice was gentle. Her eyes, when he looked up, were calm and accepting, inviting him to tell her all about himself. Inviting him into her life. Inviting him to trust in her.

Maybe if he showed that he trusted her she would learn to trust in him.

But at what cost?

Time slowed down. Around them people chatted. A gondola with no passengers on board passed outside their window. Was the gondolier going home to his family? To his wife and children?

'I never knew...' He paused, unable to finish the sentence, unable to say the words *my father*.

'But you wanted to?'

'Up until I was nine years old I believed he would one day come and live with us. My mother said that he would.'

'But he didn't?'

'No. My mother told me when I was nine that she had met a man and we moved into his apartment in Rome. I kept asking her... What about my father? How would he find us now that we had moved? She told me that he would never come. That he didn't even know that I existed...and she had no way of letting him know.'

'Who *is* your father?'

A tight cord wrapped around his throat. He struggled to swallow. 'Apart from his name... Paul...I don't know.'

Her fingers curled a fraction more tightly on his hands.

Her cool skin was a balm to the heat burning in his stomach.

'My mother was eighteen when they met. He was an American student, travelling through Europe. He and my mother met at a music festival in Rome. They spent the weekend together. It was only after he had left that my mother realised that she was pregnant.'

'Did she try to find him?'

'She knew his first name—Paul—but couldn't remember his last name. She hadn't thought it was important. They were teenagers having fun.'

'It must have been tough for your mum, bringing you up alone.'

'We didn't have a lot of money. Her work was precarious. She worked as a model; but never got the big-earning jobs. My grandmother lived with us too, on and off.'

Memories collided in his stomach. He sucked in some air at the punches they delivered. The constant worry of not having money. His mother's mood swings. The sobs coming from behind the bathroom door at night. Her red-rimmed eyes clashing with her cheery smile when she walked from the bathroom in a cloud of steam. Pretending, burying, denying.

Those memories pushed upwards, heavy in his chest, spewing from his throat.

'When I was younger she never dated. Now I know she was hoping that my father would return. That by some miracle he would find her. On the tenth anniversary of them meeting she even went to the concert venue. Hoping he'd be there. She told me all this when I was older. All night she stood outside. Hoping. But he never came. After that she gave up hoping and started dating other men. She ping-ponged from one relationship to another. Within weeks of her meeting a new boyfriend we would move in with him. We even moved countries so that she could be with them. Invariably she would either end the rela-

tionship or behave so appallingly that her boyfriend would end it.'

He took a gulp of his wine.

'When I was sixteen she broke it off with a
man who was perfect for her, who loved her. She
would have had a good life with him. I knew she
was fond of him so I was angry, frustrated. We
had a massive argument which ended in her admitting that she had never got over losing my father. She claims that she fell in love with him the
moment she first saw him, queuing ahead of her
at the entrance to the concert, but didn't realise
it until after he had left. She says that she's still
in love with him.'

The waiter came once again and glanced at
their table, clearly confused as to why their plates
were still practically untouched.

Matteo asked him to take them away.

When the waiter had gone, Emma gave him
a wide-eyed look of disbelief. 'She's still in love
with him? Even though they only spent a weekend together?'

He couldn't blame her for her incredulous tone.
'I know. I told her she was living a fantasy. She
disagreed. But ever since that night when we
argued she hasn't dated again. She says that she
now realises she was always trying to replicate
her love for my father with other men. And that

it will never work because her heart is still with my father.'

'That's so sad. For her and you.' Her tone was sombre, sincere.

He shrugged. 'These things happen. She was a good mother in most respects... She looked so young that when I was a boy people assumed she was my older sister. That my grandmother was my mother.'

'Did you mind that people thought that?'

He *had* minded. A lot. Not only had he not known his father but people had constantly assumed the wrong person was his mother.

'It didn't help that we constantly moved, and my mother stood out compared to the other mothers. She was so much younger. She never managed to become part of a community. It always felt like we were on the outside.'

'I'm sorry.'

'I'm not. It taught me that I needed to be self-reliant. It gave me a determination to succeed.'

'And you *have* succeeded.'

Had he? Until this week he had thought he had. But now all those certainties about what he wanted in life were crumbling.

'Perhaps.'

'I'm sorry you never got to know your dad, Matteo. For your mum to love him so much still he must be a special person. And I'm sorry your childhood was so disruptive as a result…it's all really sad.'

He drew back into his own chair.

It *was* sad.

He had never thought of it like that before.

Instead he had shut himself down. He had lived only for protecting himself against poverty, against allowing others to hurt him again. Had he been living in an emotional vacuum all that time?

Emma was waiting for him to respond. He could not meet her eye.

He tugged at his shirt-cuffs. 'I got used to it. Lots of children grow up in one-parent homes.'

'Yes…but it sounds like your mum was always searching for happiness. That must have had an impact on you.'

He closed his eyes for a moment. But the darkness did nothing to assail the memories of the summer when he'd turned twelve.

Francesco.

In the corridor outside his Turin apartment. Begging his mother not to leave. Clinging to him. Feeling Francesco's arms so tight around his torso that he couldn't breathe.

Francesco begging his mother not to take him away. Not the boy he considered his own son.

Panic had gripped him.

He'd been terrified that she would take him

away. Equally terrified that she might leave without him.

Now his throat felt raw with emotion. A separate entity from the rest of his body. As if all his emotions were concentrated there.

He wanted this conversation to end.

Now.

It had gone too far.

He didn't want to talk about his past any longer. 'I guess.'

The only indication that Emma wasn't convinced by his answer was an almost imperceptible narrowing of her eyes before she asked, 'Are you close to your mum now?'

Their argument when he was sixteen had left them both raw and bruised, but in the years since they had formed a truce. A truce based on burying the past. Ignoring past hurts. It had worked for them. Hadn't it?

'Yes. And with *Nonnina*—my grandmother...'

Glad of a way to break the heavy emotion bouncing between them, he smiled and added, 'Even if she *does* bring home waifs and strays.'

Her eyes duelled with his for a few seconds. A smile of tenderness lightly lifted her full lips. But then it faded. 'You're lucky to have them.'

Her words were spoken with a gentle wistfulness.

It pulled him up short.

Despite all their faults—his mother's tempestuous nature, his grandmother's anger on behalf of the poor that so often got her into trouble with the authorities—he *was* lucky to have them in his life. He had never stopped to appreciate just how much before now.

'Yes, I guess I *am* lucky,' he said.

He had family.

Emma had none.

A wave of protectiveness towards her swept through him. What was the future going to bring her? Who would look out for her? Who was going to be in her corner, fighting for her, supporting her, cheering her on?

Who was going to ask the hard questions? Challenge her?

'Will you go back to ballet?'

Emma's fingers trailed lightly against the rosemary growing in a small green metal pot to the side of their table. She prodded the pot with a finger until it tilted.

Why on earth was he asking her about ballet? Hearing him speak about his childhood had brought a feeling of closeness and understanding between them. She didn't want it to end. Talking about ballet was the last thing she wanted to do.

'Where does your mum live now?'

'In Puglia. What about you going back to ballet?'

He wasn't going to let it go. The challenge in his eyes told her so. Why was it so difficult to answer his question? Was it because of the intimacy that had been growing all morning? Their earlier argument? Their laughter in the mask studio? Matteo opening up just now about his past? The connection, closeness, *confidence* of his admissions? The fact that he trusted her enough to share his past?

It was thrilling, yet terrifying. Could she ever again trust a man enough to reveal what was in her heart?

For a few seconds she hesitated on the brink of telling him everything—how she was terrified of dreaming again. Scared to dare risking her heart to ballet, to a man. Her fear of it all going wrong yet again.

'Go back to ballet? Why should I? It's in my past.'

Much too intelligent soft brown eyes held hers. 'It doesn't have to be.'

Her gaze shifted to the elegant middle-aged couple at the next table, who were leaving amidst much chatter and laughter. The woman was searching under the table for forgotten items. The man was patting his pockets. Mentally checking his belongings.

'I want it to be in my past.'

'Why?'

His quietly spoken question crept through the cage of fear engulfing her heart, and the tender expression in his eyes released—just a little—the burden of failure clogging her throat.

'Because it hurts too much to think about what I lost.'

'But you could create a new future in ballet through teaching, Pilates instruction, choreography… Maybe you can find something even better than you had ever hoped for.'

'And what if I don't? What if it only brings up bad memories or I fail again?'

'You have to take risks in life, otherwise it will be a life half lived.'

He was wrong. Risks…daring to dream…led to bitter disappointment, despair. She would prefer to live a life of caution, knowing just how cruel life could be, rather than have every hope wiped out again in the blink of an eye—in the seconds it took to fall down some stairs, the seconds it took for a policeman to rap at your door.

'I want to focus on my career.'

'You can have more than your career.'

'Seriously? *You*, Mr Workaholic, are telling *me* that?'

'Nobody said I was perfect.'

From where she was sitting he seemed pretty perfect to her. His open-necked blue shirt hinted at the golden-skinned muscular chest beneath, and

long, elegant fingers were toying with his glass...
toying with her heart.

'So are you saying that *you* might open up your
life to other things?'

Matteo rocked back in his chair, answering her
question with a brief shrug.

Irked by his nonchalance, feeling a desire to
provoke him, she asked, 'How about a relationship?'

He leaned forward in his chair, his hand once
again twisting and twisting the stem of his glass.
'Maybe, if... *Dio*, I don't know.'

He threw himself back into his chair. Raised a
hand in the air in exasperation.

Outside, the sun disappeared behind a white
puffball cloud. The shaft of light that had been
highlighting the chestnut depths of his hair, the
golden tone of his skin, disappeared.

The chatter of the other diners dimmed in her
ears. Her heartbeat drummed against her chest.

'She'll be a lucky person.'

His eyes searched hers. 'Will she?'

She bit down on her impulse to laugh, to tease
him. To ask him glibly why *any* woman wouldn't
feel lucky to be the partner of a gorgeous, intelligent, kind man.

But to do so would be a disservice.

He deserved more from her. He deserved the
truth. Not some superficial answer.

She shuffled forward in her chair, leaned towards him.

Her eyes locked with his and her heart was now in her throat, her tummy coiling tighter and tighter.

'Only if you open your heart to her.'

Her answer came out in a whisper.

He blinked as he took in her words. And then his gaze became one of tender intensity.

He was looking at her in a way that no man had ever stared at her. As though she was the only person alive, ever to have existed.

Her heart sank back down into her chest and exploded into a million droplets of pleasure, of wistfulness, of emotional desire for the man sitting opposite her.

The waiter appeared at her side, a large white circular porcelain plate in each hand. She jumped in alarm. For a moment she had forgotten where she was.

When the waiter had left, she dubiously prodded her risotto with her fork. It was ink-black in colour.

Not what she had expected.

She glanced over to Matteo.

'Your first time having black cuttlefish risotto?' he asked with a teasing grin.

'It's so strange-looking—not exactly appetising.'

'Try it—it's delicious.'

'It looks like something spewed up by a volcano.'

He shook his head, laughing. 'Trust me...try it.'

She picked up some grains with her fork. Stared at it for a while and then tentatively popped it in her mouth. Salt. The taste of the sea. Garlic. She tried another forkful. And then another. She lowered her fork with a sigh.

'Oh, wow. That's *so* good. I'll have to add it to my list of favourite Italian food.'

'You like Italian food?'

She took another forkful and answered his grin with her own smile. 'I *adore* Italian food.'

He spiralled some of the spaghetti from his soft-shelled crab, langoustines and tomato sauce dish before saying, 'You'll have to come back and visit again some time.'

He spoke as though his invitation was sincere. As though he actually believed it would be possible.

She hid her confusion behind a teasing smile. 'Maybe. Although it's much more likely that the next time we meet I'll be at the end of a walkie-talkie while you are swanning around some glitzy event in London.'

His eyes twinkled. 'I'll make sure to wave to you.'

She gave a sigh and shook her head. 'We're really from different worlds.'

'No. Same world. Same problems and doubts.'

Hardly. He was rich and successful. She was a runaway bride without a job or a home. But now was not the time to point those facts out. Now was about forgetting about the past *and* the future.

'If I'm in a good mood I'll make sure to send you over a martini with lemon peel instead of champagne.'

He paused in twirling his pasta. 'You remembered?'

Her heart danced with pleasure at being the focus of his smile. 'Of course.'

He reached over and stole some of her risotto. 'And I'll tell the host just how incredible his event co-coordinator is.'

She playfully pulled her plate out of his reach. 'Make sure to add that I'm deserving of a bonus.'

As they ate the rest of their meal they spoke about food. Matteo grew increasingly appalled on hearing Emma's description of her boarding school fare.

As the waiter cleared away their main course Matteo said, 'Tinned sausages, gravy and potatoes…? It sounds horrible.'

Emma gave a shudder. 'Trust me, it tasted even worse.'

Matteo frowned hard, as though her boarding school's food was an affront to all humanity. When the waiter had left, he said, 'I will cook for you some day…to make up for all that terrible food.'

At first they smiled, both enjoying the teasing. But then their smiles faded. And Emma felt her cheeks grow hot. Her entire body, in fact.

His eyes darkened.

Silence pulsated between them.

He leaned towards her.

Her heart wobbled and quivered and pinched in her chest.

Serious, intent, masculine eyes devoured her, travelling down over her mouth, her throat, lingering on the pull of her jumper over her breasts.

'I have a surprise I want to show you.'

Her stomach tumbled at the low, sensual timbre of his voice.

She nodded.

Followed him on giddy legs when he stood.

Outside, she didn't object when he reached for her hand. His touch sent her heart careening around her body. The ever-growing ache in her body was physically hurting now.

Ten minutes later she found herself at the rear street entrance to Ca' Divina.

Puzzled, she asked, 'What about my surprise?'

Opening the door, Matteo unbuttoned his coat and gave her a mischievous smile. 'A little patience, please.'

Emma paused at the door, thrown by how

much she wanted to be here. In Ca' Divina. Alone with him.

Inside, she followed him up to the second floor. At the end of the corridor, past all the bedrooms, Matteo pressed firmly against the pale-blue-painted wall. A hidden door popped open. Emma gave a gasp of surprise.

Behind the door was a staircase, a skylight high above it filling the wood-panelled stairway with warm light. Dense, peaceful air filled the enclosed space.

At the top of the stairs he opened a dark wood-panelled door and led her out onto a flat red-brick roof terrace. Large bay trees in pots were dotted around the vast space; all-weather outdoor furniture stood at the centre.

She moved about the terrace, her hand lifting silently, a huge beam of excitement on her face. Pointing to St Mark's Basilica, Campanile San Giorgio Maggiore in the south, the Rialto Bridge to the east, the utter beauty of the Grand Canal below.

She left out a happy, thrilled laugh. 'This is so *incredible*.'

Matteo leaned against the stone balustrade overlooking the canal. Watching her. Amused. 'I told you to trust me.'

She was feeling decidedly giddy. Especially with the way he was looking at her. Interested. More than interested. With a definite spark.

the bags to the floor. Her hand touched against the soft brown leather of the tub chair in front of his desk.

'Eventually. Thanks to a lot of pointing and hand gestures. Although at one point it looked a distinct possibility that we were about to have a fish that resembled a deflated soccer ball rather than mussels for lunch.'

His laughter tripped along her veins. Her fingers squeezed the soft leather of the chair. For a moment it felt as if gravity didn't apply to her. Dizzying memories came of their heads colliding in bed last night and Matteo pretending to be concussed. She had tested that pretence by slowly kissing him, until he had groaned in capitulation and tossed her onto her back.

She should go and make lunch. Her forfeit for being the first to beg in a game this morning.

His laughter died. And now his intense gaze wrapped her in a bubble of glorious hope.

'I missed you.'

She looked away. Unable to cope with the sincerity in his eyes. 'I doubt that—you were engrossed in your work just now.'

With a playful grin Matteo stood and walked towards her.

Anticipation tickled her insides. She was not going to blush. Or think about what he had done to her body last night. How she had moaned as his mouth had travelled down her body, staying far too long at her breasts.

He stood over her, his grin now plain sexy, thanks to the heat in his eyes. His scent rocketed through her senses, leaving her temporarily stunned and having to fight the temptation to close her eyes, sigh, lean into him.

'You're determined not to believe a word I say, aren't you?'

She had to brazen it out. Not give any hint that last night had changed anything. Pretend that it *hadn't* left her wanting to crawl right into his skin and know him better than anyone else in this world.

'As I've told you already, it's the new me… tough, independent.'

He sat on the corner of his desk, his long legs in exquisite navy wool trousers spread out before him. Earlier, before she had left for the market, he had kissed her in the kitchen as they'd tidied up after a late breakfast. His hips had moulded against hers, which had been pushed against a kitchen cabinet, and her fingers had marvelled at the smooth texture of the fabric of his trousers and the strength of the muscle and hardness beneath.

'How about we put that alleged toughness to the test?'

There was a dangerous glint in his eye.

She pointed to the grocery bags on the floor. 'What about lunch?'

He gave her a *you're not so tough now, are you?* grin and beckoned her forward with the curl of a finger. 'Come here.'

His command was spoken in a low, husky voice. His smile had disappeared. His eyes devoured her. Her heart thumped and pounded and ricocheted around her chest. Desire left her faint with the craving to be in his arms again.

She stopped two paces away.

When he didn't react, she edged a little closer. And then a little closer again.

No reaction.

He was torturing her.

She edged forward. Need driving her on.

She came to a stop less than six inches away.

Other than devouring her with his eyes, he didn't respond.

Inside, she yelled for him to touch her, to kiss her again. To reach out for her. To complete her.

On the outside she didn't move a muscle. Determined not to be the first to move. Determined to prove—to herself as much as him—that she was tough. Determined to believe that she could walk away from him whenever it suited her.

He reached forward and slowly drew down the zip of her padded jacket. Need pooled in her core.

She wriggled a little, trying to ease its beautiful pressure.

'*Mi piace come baci.*'

Oh, Lord, she was going to lose her mind. Did he *have* to speak in such a low, sexy whisper? She swallowed hard, her throat's tightness an alarming contrast to the loose panic of her heart.

'What does that mean?'

'*Mi piace come baci*—I love how you kiss me.'

'Oh.'

His hand snaked beneath her jacket. Then a finger curled around the belt loop of her jeans and yanked her between his legs. He leaned in towards her, only inches separating them.

The heat of his body encircled her, sending her hazy thoughts off into recess.

'*Adoro come mi fai sentire.*'

He really wasn't playing fair. 'What does *that* mean?'

'I love the way you make me feel.'

Oh, crikey, she was going down. And fast.

Despite herself, she closed the gap between them. Her hip inched towards his lap. Her mouth was almost touching his.

'*Ho bisogno di te.*'

His breath smelt of mint, of toothpaste. His fingers were slowly untucking her tee shirt from her jeans. Slow, unrushed movements, sensual in their laziness. Sensual in the knowing confidence that she wouldn't object. That this was exactly what she wanted.

'And that?'

His head angled perfectly to align with her mouth. 'I need you.'

With a groan she landed her lips on his. She wanted to cry out when he didn't respond at first. But quickly she realised he was happy for her to be in control now. For her to lead the way. She captured his head in her hands and deepened the kiss. Then her hands moved down to his, and silently she urged him to touch her.

Within minutes she was standing before him, her jacket and tee shirt gone, only her jeans and red satin bra remaining.

They made love on the floor.

Hot, desperate, addictive love.

Knowing their time was running out.

Outside his bedroom window darkness had settled on the city. The ball was in less than two hours. He should wake Emma. But she was lying beside him, her arms sprawled over her head on the pillow, the blankets at her waist, and he wanted more time to watch her. Watch the rise and fall of her ribcage, the perfect globes of her breasts. Watch the invitingly open lush cupid's bow shape of her mouth, the flush on her porcelain skin.

She was staggeringly beautiful.

And sleeping with her had been the most heart-wrenching, honest and tender experience of his life.

She was a gentle lover. Almost shy. And she responded to his every touch with wonder shining brilliantly from her eyes.

They had spent the past twenty-four hours in each other's arms. Ravenous for one another.

He was in love with her.

And he was lost as to what to do.

She said she didn't want a relationship, to love again. But with time would she change her mind?

And, even if she did, what if she said she did love him only to walk away one day? After he had given her his heart.

He was in love with her.

But he would never tell her.

Because to do so would mean that she would have the power to leave him.

And that he could never cope with.

Emma stabbed her brush into the almond-coloured eyeshadow. The fine powder crumbled beneath the force. She swept the brush along one closed lid. When she was done she stared at the reflection of the bedroom in the dressing table mirror. Why did she feel she no longer belonged there?

She closed both eyes and grimaced as her heart

floated downwards into her stomach, where it rocked to the nervous tension already there.

She had to stop thinking.

Get through the next few hours.

Now should only be about appreciating her remaining precious hours with Matteo.

She opened her eyes in time to catch the already ajar bedroom door opening more fully in the mirror's reflection.

Matteo, dressed in a tuxedo, stepped into the room.

Goosebumps ran along her skin.

She pulled the edges of her dressing gown closer together.

Her heart, her body, her mind were all alert to him. Silently calling out to him.

Unspoken words stole into the room and beat in the air between them.

Matteo walked towards her. Her pulse raced faster with each step. He came to a stop directly behind her, a hand touching against her loose hair.

'I'll help you dress.'

She yearned to lean back, to have his fingers once again bury themselves in her hair, to have his fingertips caress her skull, her neck, her back.

Start pretending, Emma. Come on. Start acting tough. Don't you dare start believing in dreams again.

'Thanks, but it has a side zip. I'll manage by myself.'

His eyes narrowed before he turned and walked to the antique tapestry-covered chair beside her bed. 'I'll wait while you get ready.'

She wanted to say no. That to have him watch would be too intimate. That it was what somebody in a relationship would do. That it wasn't what they were about.

But she couldn't find the right words of protest.

Her dress was lying on the bed. A pink strapless floor-length silk gown, shot through with threads of peach and gold.

'Turn away.'

Engulfing the small chair he was sitting in, Matteo flashed a hand through his still damp hair. '*Per carità!* You cannot be serious. After the past twenty-four hours?'

'This is different.'

'Why?'

Because I couldn't bear to have you watch me... couldn't bear the vulnerability I would feel.

'I don't know, but it is.'

Throwing both hands up in the air, Matteo stood and walked to the bedroom window.

Emma quickly peeled off her dressing gown and stepped into the dress.

'You have a beautiful body.'

Her head shot up. Matteo still had his back to

her. She pulled up the bodice to cover her bare breasts.

She gave a huff of disbelief. 'Hardly—in comparison to the naked models you see all the time.'

He twisted his head around—not enough to watch her, but enough to mark his presence, his control of the mood in the room. 'I don't care about other women, what they look like. I'm telling you that your body is mesmerising.'

There was more than a hint of annoyance to his voice.

She gave a laugh, needing to keep this conversation light and teasing. 'I believe you.'

He turned fully, his jaw set hard, a warning look flashing in his eyes. 'I never lie.'

She looked down and fiddled with her zip, wishing she *could* believe him. Wishing life hadn't taught her not to trust what anyone said.

She'd intended not to react, not to say anything, but when she looked up and into his eyes she heard herself say in a low voice, 'Is that a promise?'

Silence fell on the room. Matteo did not move a muscle. Dark and brooding, with the sharp contours of his athletic body clearly defined by the bespoke slim-cut tailoring of his tuxedo, he stared at her with an intensity that had her heart pounding in her ears, goosebumps serrating her skin.

He lifted his head in a gesture she had thought was one of arrogance when they'd first met, but now she knew it was one of intense pride and honour. 'Of course.'

She wanted to believe him. Not to be so scarred by her past. She wanted to walk to him and kiss him tenderly. She wanted to find adequate words to express the emotion pirouetting in her heart. She wanted to cancel the ball and spend these last hours alone with him, in his arms.

But to do so would mean allowing herself to hope, believe, trust, dream again.

Things she could never do.

So instead she fluttered her hands through the heavy silk of the gown's skirt and gave a single pirouette. 'Well, Prince Charming, am I okay to go to the ball?'

Matteo walked towards her, the seriousness in his eyes fading to amusement. A smile appeared on his mouth. '*Sei bellissima.* You are beautiful.'

The orchestra played 'The Blue Danube' and hundreds of masked faces twirled and spun around Matteo in the gilt and frescoed ballroom.

But he only searched for one: the delicate golden wired half-mask Emma had chosen in the atelier yesterday morning.

He smiled as Mrs Xue spoke excitedly of her trip to Verona from behind her full-faced *volto* mask, stark white with gilding around the eyes. The beauty of the Basilica… The pictures she'd taken of Juliet's Balcony… All the while he was searching, searching, searching. Needing to see Emma. Suddenly wondering how he was going to let her go.

And then he saw her. Moving towards him in the arms of Mr Xue.

She danced as though she was walking on air—fluidly, elegantly, joyfully. Her long hair lifted and bounced behind her. Those she passed turned around and stared in her direction. Captivated. Her dress sparkled beneath the lights of the Murano glass chandeliers running down the centre of the ballroom, her mask spun with gold adding to the pull of her beauty.

The music came to a stop and he led Mrs Xue towards them. He bowed to Mrs Xue and held out his hand to Emma. Silently inviting her to dance.

Below her mask her mouth gave a polite smile, but there was unrest in her eyes.

They danced slowly, but then the tempo quickened.

They danced on, to the uplifting music, but second by second her body grew stiffer in his arms. Her back arched. Her hand in his was tense.

Inside, a part of him was dying. All of a sudden he was incapable of speaking to her—even as her boss, never mind her lover. He wanted to hear her laughter. To feel that world-altering connection again. But no words came. He struggled even to look at her. It hurt too much. To know what he was about to lose. All he could do was stare blindly into the distance. Focus on the warmth and softness of her hand in his. How perfect it felt in his grasp. A perfect fit. Enticing. Nourishing. *Home.*

He heard himself ask, 'Is everything okay?'

Her response was equally polite. Impersonal. Strained. 'Yes, of course.'

He glanced down quickly and then away. Felt a dragging pain in his heart. As though it was bound by two gondolas travelling in opposite directions on a dark foggy night.

'What time do you have to leave tomorrow?'

She spoke with an edge. Was she dreading tomorrow as much as he was?

'I need to be at the airport for nine.'

She tucked her head down so that he couldn't see her eyes, but her fingers curled even tighter around his hand.

'So early?'

He grimaced at the regret in her voice. 'Unfortunately.'

Another couple moved too close to them and the woman collided hard against Emma. She gave a gasp of surprise.

The woman began to apologise, the heat in her cheeks below her half-mask showing her distress.

Emma held out her hand and touched the woman's bare arm. 'I'm fine, don't worry.'

The warmth and kindness of Emma's reassurance shifted something inside him. The way she'd touched the woman—empathetic, dignified—the gentleness of her tone. *This* was the type of woman he wanted to spend his life with. Centred. Compassionate. Caring.

He couldn't let her go.

The couple moved away.

Emma's eyes met his. Sad. Determined.

'I'll leave at the same time as you tomorrow.'

Confused, he pulled back from her. 'Why?'

Her gaze moved to the centre of his throat. He swallowed hard. Remembered her lips and tongue swirling over that tender skin at sunrise this morning.

'I've booked a hotel for my final days here in Venice.'

Not understanding, he said, 'I had assumed that you would stay in Ca' Divina.'

The hand resting on his arm tightened for a moment before her touch grew slack. 'That wouldn't be right.'

'Why?'

She shrugged. 'You've done enough for me.'

Her voice was impatient.

What was going on? Why was she springing this on him now?

Something hot and angry stirred in his stomach. She was walking out on him. He had fallen in love with her and she was walking away. He had thought she would stay. That he would leave for New York knowing that she was still in Ca' Divina. While Emma had remained there they would have had a connection. He would have had a legitimate reason to call her and see how she was doing. He had even envisaged her sleeping in his bed.

But instead she was walking away. Walking away from his home. From his hospitality. Walking away from their week together and the memories contained within the walls of Ca' Divina. Walking away from *him*.

And it didn't seem to be of any significance to her.

Anger leached from his stomach. Poisoned the rest of his body. His jaw locked. Every muscle tensed.

'Why didn't you tell me that you would be leaving?'

Her head snapped up. 'Why should I have?'

'Because it would have been polite.'

Those beautiful slender shoulders rose again. In a casual throwaway gesture that cut him in two.

'What does it matter when I leave? I thought you'd be relieved.'

The poison was in his throat. In his mind. He wanted to yell. But he forced his voice to remain cool, detached.

'Relieved?'

Emma couldn't read Matteo. There was anger in his eyes. But his voice was businesslike. Remote.

'It's time we both move on.'

She could hear herself speak…in the voice of another person. A person who was relaxed about moving on. Happy and accepting. While in truth, inside, her ribs felt as if they were going to snap under the pressure of sadness building in her chest.

Matteo gave an impatient sigh. And then fiercely, begrudgingly, he said, 'Come and work for me in Milan.'

She laughed out of confusion. A short, bitter noise.

'Work for you?'

She heard Matteo curse under his breath and then he yanked off his black half-mask.

The tips of his cheeks were red, agitated. 'I need a replacement for my event co-ordinator whilst she's on maternity leave.'

She wanted to cry. But instead she said dismissively, 'I can't work for you, Matteo.'

The redness in his cheeks spread. He lowered his head and eyeballed her. 'Why not?'

Because I will only fall in love with you even more.

She looked away, irritation layering on top of

her sadness and confusion. How dared he speak to her in such a demanding tone?

She gritted her teeth, yanked off her own mask and said in an ice-cold tone, 'Because it would be too awkward—we've slept together, for heaven's sake. Anyway, I need to get back to London. Sort out accommodation, a job...I need to focus on my career. I want to go home.'

Those brown eyes were no longer soft, but as hard as rain-parched earth. 'And London is your home?'

A lifetime of hurt bubbled inside her. For the first time ever she felt a true, raw need to be tough erupting.

She inched closer to him and looked him steadily in the eye. 'Yes. London is my home. It's where my career will be.'

He nodded, but she could tell from the hard determination in his eyes that he wasn't going to leave it without a fight.

'I want you to stay. Give it six months. You don't have to commit to anything permanent. Think about what great experience you will gain. How it will look on your CV.'

Incredulously, she asked, 'You want me to give up my life in London?'

Those eyes, parched of emotion, held hers. 'I don't want you to go... I like what we have. You don't have an apartment or a job in London. Why not move to Milan? I have an apartment in Porta Venezia you can use.'

She was *so* sick of being used. First her parents. Then her ex. Now Matteo wanted to use her for his own ends. In the workplace and no doubt in the bedroom.

She planted her feet firmly on the ground. She was sick of dancing with him. Sick with herself for thinking he might be different.

She snatched her hand out of his. Jerked her other hand away from his arm. 'Because it's *my* life. I'm not some…bit on the side. I'm not interested in having a relationship with you for a few months. I can't function like that. And, frankly, I'm insulted that you would think that I would be happy being your…your kept mistress.'

He stepped closer to her and lowered his head. 'I'm asking you to *work* for me—nothing else. Why are you making such a big deal about it?' he demanded in a furious voice.

She jerked away.

What was he saying?

If he didn't want to sleep with her, was he saying that he had no interest in her? No desire for her? How could that be when attraction sizzled between them?

Or was she mistaken?

Was this all one-sided?

Pride called for her not to speak. But her pain,

her hurt, her confusion were too great. 'Are you saying that you don't *want* to sleep with me again? That it would be a business arrangement only?'

He shook his head. Lifted his arms in exasperation. Confusion drifted across his features before he asked furiously, 'What do *you* want, Emma?'

Tears were forming at the back of her throat. With a cry she whispered, 'I don't know. I don't *know*, Matteo. But I certainly don't want this.'

CHAPTER TEN

EMMA RAN FROM the ball, the music and lights fading with every step, and tugged on her coat. The freezing night air was an affront to her hot anger.

She darted down the nearest side street.

Move to Milan? Work for him? Be his paid lover?

Hurt, fury, and a feeling of utter naïvety all twisted wildly in her stomach, moving upwards like a tornado until they gripped her throat. She could barely breathe.

Her ankle throbbed.

Blindly she hobbled along the maze of *calli*, cursing her exquisite pale pink Marco sandals, not made for cobbled streets. She had the vague hope that she'd finally stumble upon a recognisable landmark. But she didn't care that she was lost. Or that there were few people out at this time of night.

She wanted to be alone.

She wanted to try to understand why his proposal had stung so deeply.

She wanted to understand why it felt as though the past week had been nothing but a lie.

The connection she had thought they'd shared had been nothing more than a delusion on her part.

Their relationship was nothing more than a physical attraction for him.

Not an emotional connection.

Not the deep understanding of another person—the ability to read their needs and respond to them.

After everything she had said, how could he think that she'd be happy to uproot her life, turn it upside down for a man? A man who said he never wanted a permanent relationship.

How on earth would she manage to walk away from him after six months, a year, when it already felt so gut-wrenchingly awful to face the thought of him leaving tomorrow?

And the most infuriating, feet-stamping, tantrum-inducing part of all of this was that she didn't *want* to be in love.

But she was.

She loved him.

How could she be so stupid?

How could she be so foolish to fall in love with a man who had always said he didn't want to be in a relationship?

How could she be so reckless to allow herself to get hurt again?

On a humpback bridge she came to a stop at the

apex and stared along the silent flowing water of the dark canal below.

It was snowing. How hadn't she noticed before now? Slowly swirling fat flakes dropped onto her outstretched palm. The flakes melted instantly against the heat of her skin. Just as the connection, the trust, the respect, the feeling deep in her bones that she had met her soulmate had melted tonight.

Pain radiated from her ankle. Cramping her calf muscle. She curled her toes and lifted her leg to rotate her ankle. Balanced on one leg, she wobbled and almost fell over.

She wanted to scream at life to give her a break.

She needed to get home.

Out of the cold.

But it wasn't home.

When had she even started to consider it as such?

Emptiness swept over her. She twisted away from the canal and tottered down the steep slope of the bridge on numb feet. Overwhelmed at the thought of a future without Matteo.

Before, she had clung to the hope that she would have memories to sustain her. Memories of a kind, generous, empathetic man.

Now she was no longer certain if that was who he really was.

Had be just been playing her? To get her into his bed?

She slipped and lurched along a narrow *calle*. The tall buildings either side seemed to be bearing down on her. Echoing the thin, stiletto fall of her footsteps.

The snow continued to fall.

A church bell rang out nearby.

She followed its sound.

And gasped when she walked into San Marco Square, blanketed in a thin layer of snow. Only a few solo, silent mysterious figures traversed the square, disappearing and appearing again from the arcades of the *procuratie*.

A sharp pain gripped her ribs. Forcing the air from her lungs.

She wanted Matteo to be here.

To witness the beauty of the square with her.

To hold her hand. To pull her tight against his body. To warm her. To hold her safe. To hold her for ever.

She turned her back on the square.

She knew her way back to Ca' Divina from here.

She would sleep and leave early tomorrow. And start her life afresh.

Her tears were pointless. She swiped at them, every muscle in her body hardening. She was furious with herself. For every single decision she had taken this past week.

* * *

She woke to feel her heart pounding a slow, heavy beat. Without opening her eyes she knew he was there. The adrenaline swamping her muscles, the tingle on her skin, the alertness in her brain—all told her that he was in the room.

Should she open her eyes? Confront him? Perhaps even manage to say goodbye in a civilised manner.

But would she run the risk of falling prey to his chemistry? To her weakness when she was around him?

She ground her teeth together. Annoyed with herself.

She snapped her eyes open.

He was sitting in the blue floral tapestry chair beside her bed, his bow tie undone, a dark shadow on his jawline and shadows below his eyes. Eyes that were studying her as if he was trying to stare into her soul.

She wanted to pull the covers over her head. To turn away from the awful compulsion invading every cell in her body to fold back the covers and silently ask him into her bed. To lose herself in him again.

Instead she pulled herself upright and hugged her knees against her.

They sat in silence. He held her gaze but she

looked away. Her lips clamped shut. Her teeth aching. She was determined not to say anything.

'Why did you run out of the ball?'

His voice was low, gruff, tired.

She drew her knees tighter into her chest. Disappointment grabbed at her heart and then an even stronger, more breath-stealing sadness yanked at her chest. Her jaw ached with the pressure of trying not to let out a cry.

She swallowed time and time again, but her upset was still clear when she asked, 'Do you know me so little that you have to ask that question?'

He leaned back in his chair and folded one leg over the other. The cold, hard expression of a CEO going in for the kill was on his face. 'You embarrassed me in front of my clients.'

She jerked back against the pillows of the bed, shock and anger erupting from her. 'Are you *serious*? Is that all that you care about?'

He leapt from his chair. Tense and dark. Prowled beside her bed. His shoulders bunched tight. A hand tore through his hair in disbelief. 'I needed you there. As my partner. And you left me.'

There was raw pain in his voice. Distressed pride in his eyes.

Speechless, she stared at him. Her mouth opening and closing. She had hurt him. How, she had no idea. But she had. And her heart ached. Ached for him. Ached for the mess they both were in.

'What's going on, Matteo?'

He glanced briefly at her. Flinging exasperation and anger at her. 'I can't stay here. Let's go for a walk. I'll meet you downstairs in twenty minutes.'

She moved forward. Trying to reach him. 'Why?'

Matteo, already at the bedroom door, twisted around to her, the ache inside him shooting out in furious words. 'Because we need to talk and I'm not doing it here.'

He gestured impatiently to the bed and then stared at her. Defying her not to understand how it was too painful a reminder of their hours spent together making slow, passionate love time and time again.

Too painful a reminder of how it was the way they had first met. In the intimacy of a bed. Inches apart. Staring into the eyes of a stranger. Who wasn't a stranger at all.

Anger flowing through his veins, Matteo stormed into his bedroom. After a rushed shower he dressed in charcoal wool trousers and a light grey shirt, both suitable for the long journey ahead in his private plane to New York. He should have packed yesterday evening. But instead he had spent that time in bed with Emma.

He slammed some clothes into his suitcase with

a carelessness that made him wonder if he was losing his mind.

Hurt convulsed through him. He steadied himself by locking his knees against the side of the bed. Doubled over above the open suitcase. Pain ripping through the centre of him.

She had walked out on him.

He had tried to reach out to her. He had given her a solution that would keep them together for a while. A solution that gave him some hope of a possible future together.

And she had thrown it back in his face.

Walked out on him.

Just like every other person he had ever been foolish enough to allow into his life, to have loved, had done in the past.

They walked in silence through alleyways and squares, over the Rialto Bridge into the *sestiere* of San Marco. The city of bridges, the city of romance, had never looked so beautiful and serene in the early-morning light, with a thin blanket of snow covering the city.

With few people about, they almost had the city to themselves.

In the pink-tinged dawn light, a blue sky was beginning to unfurl.

Words tumbled in Matteo's brain. He wanted to lash out. Pain was burning in his gut. In his heart.

In his mind. He pulled his woollen hat down further over his ears, lifted the collar of his coat. The fire inside him intensified the bitter pull of the outside temperature.

'I wasn't trying to insult you last night with my job offer.'

Emma upped her pace, putting distance between them. Her arms were folded tight across her padded jacket, her suede boots tramping the snow.

'I've upended my life for a man before. I'm not doing it again.'

He caught up with her as she entered Campo della Fava and pulled her to a stop. *'Per carità!* Are you serious, Emma? Are you comparing me to a man who *lied* to you? A *criminal*?'

Her blue-hatted head shook furiously. 'No… I'm not comparing you. But—'

He grabbed her by the arms and pulled her closer. Desperate for her to understand. 'I was trying to find a way for us to see each other for a while. I *like* you, Emma. I don't want us to lose contact.'

An incredulous expression grew on her face. 'You like me.'

It was not a question. More a statement of disgust.

With an angry huff she continued, 'And what happens in six months' time? In a year? Don't you think we're just going to hurt each other?'

He swallowed hard. Thrown by her fury. Her passion. Thrown by how much he longed to cup her pink-tinged cheeks and lower his lips to her mouth. To pull off her hat and lose his fingers in the soft weight of her hair. To inhale her rose scent once again. To know that she was his.

All that desire and want collided with the fear rampaging in his chest, in his heart. He grappled for words. The right words. *Any* words. He was about to put his heart on the line. Could he go through with it?

He swung away from the sight of her peppermint-toffee eyes searching his. Looking…waiting for an answer.

He marched towards the red-brick edifice of Chiesa di Santa Maria della Fava before twisting back again. 'In six months' time, a year, you might be ready for a relationship…a proper relationship.'

Her hands twisted more tightly about her waist. She lifted her chin defiantly. 'A relationship… What do you mean?'

His heart swivelled in his chest.

He felt sick.

He was about to put everything on the line.

His pride. His trust. His sworn promise to himself that he would never show any vulnerability, any need to another person.

What if she said no? Rejected him?

'I've always believed that I would never fall in love.'

He couldn't stand still. He paced up and down before her. Snow crunched under his feet.

He came to a stop. 'But I have.'

He gestured heavenwards, his head falling back. Looking for strength. His heart throbbing.

'I've fallen in love with you.'

Emotion caught in his throat. Suddenly he felt deflated. Empty.

His hands fell to his sides. 'With a woman who doesn't want to be in love.'

Paling, her expression aghast, she said incredulously, 'You've fallen in love with *me*?'

Was his admission so terrible? So unwanted? So wide of the mark from where she was at, what she wanted from this relationship?

Pain and pride slammed together in his chest. He needed to back off. Withdraw. Play it cool.

In a slow, indifferent drawl he asked, 'Is it really that horrific?'

She took a step closer to him. Her icy breath floated on the air towards him. 'Of course not. I'm not horrified. I'm just confused.'

Her hand reached out towards him. He jerked away.

For a moment she looked startled, wounded. But then she asked, 'Why didn't you want to fall in love?'

He closed his eyes. The ache in his chest was worse than the time when his mother had taken him away from Francesco. A thousand times worse. What was the point in answering her question? Did she really care?

He opened his eyes. Hazel eyes laced with tears held his gaze. In a low whisper she said, 'Matteo, please...*please*.'

He was so in love with her.

'When I was growing up my mother dated many men. Some for only weeks, others for longer...twelve, eighteen months. We would move into their homes. We would get to know their families, often their parents, brothers and sisters. I would pretend that I had a family of my own...a home. I would pretend that I had a father. But then my mother would sabotage the relationship. And it would end in one of two ways. Either the man I'd considered a father, and his parents who had treated me like a grandchild, would give in to her insistence that we move on with our lives and let us go, not fighting in any way to keep me a part of their lives. Or, if the break-up was particularly bitter, the man would throw us out onto the street.'

She moved forward and placed her hand on his chest. Just below his heart.

She looked at him and said gently, 'I'm sorry.' And then, 'There's no excusing the men who threw you out, but perhaps it was hard for those other men. Maybe they thought it would be easier for *you* if they let you go.'

Memories of Francesco clinging to him came back. If he'd been in Francesco's position, what would he have done? His throat tightened.

Her hand moved upwards. Now it was over his heart.

Her voice was hoarse. 'You think I'm doing the same thing? That I'm walking away from you?'

He was tired of pretending. Maybe if he had shown her just how upset he was when he was a child his mother would have changed. Those worthwhile father figures would have fought to stay in contact.

'Yes.'

Panic surged through Emma. 'It's not like that… I really like you. I really, *really* like you.'

She paused for breath. Her hand moved up from his heart and for a moment lingered on his jaw-line. She had an overwhelming need to lay her lips on his. To take the pain from his eyes.

'I can't imagine leaving you.'

She dropped her hand and took a step back. She looked down at the snow, tarnished now by their careless footsteps.

'But I'm scared. I've messed up so much in the past. My judgement has been so wrong. I'm scared that I'll jump into a relationship for all the wrong reasons.'

Matteo's eyes narrowed. She took some strength from the way he looked as though knowing and understanding all this was the most important thing in the world.

'I'm scared that I've fallen for you because I'm vulnerable. Because I'm confused.'

She tugged off her hat, suddenly too hot. Her brain felt as if it was sizzling. 'I came to Venice swearing that I was going to be tough and practical. Focused on my career. Determined that I was never going to dream again. And then I went and met you. And I *want* to dream. But what if it all falls apart again? I couldn't take it. I'm scared I'll lose you. That one day this dream that I'm living will fall apart.'

For the longest while Matteo stood still, drinking in what she had said. And then he moved towards her. His hand reached for her hair. Tucked some of it behind her ear.

His thumb ran down her cheek and gently he said, 'You're not ready for love. For this relationship.'

She didn't know how to answer. Tears flooded her eyes. Tears of confusion and frustration. Tears of fear. Tears of love for this man.

'Are you?'

His hand cupped her cheek. He gave a sigh. Regret and sadness deepened his eyes to soft molten toffee. 'I'm not sure,' Emma said.

She stepped back. Away from his touch. Needing to step away from telling him how much she loved him.

'Are we just fooling ourselves? Is this just about the insane chemistry we seem to share?'

He nodded, but then stopped suddenly. 'I've never felt like this with another woman.'

His gaze was now hard, direct. Deeply honest.

She sucked in a breath. 'Nor me with another man.'

His jaw worked. He ran a hand over his hat. Repositioned it. 'We need some time apart to think.'

Her stomach flipped at his words. She couldn't bear the thought of being without him. But she continued on with her sensible routine, refusing to allow her heart to have anything to say in what *had* to be a logical conversation.

'Yes.'

'I'm returning from New York on Wednesday. If we decide individually that we want to try to make this work, let's meet. I'll be at Ca' Divina at five.'

Her head spun. An army of *what if*s marched through her brain. What if this was the last time they would meet? What if he decided he didn't want to be with her? She couldn't meet him in Ca' Divina. There were too many memories there.

What if she turned up, wanting a future with him, and he didn't?

A wave of grief, rejection, embarrassment at that thought almost knocked her sideways. 'No, not there.'

'At the church in San Moisè square instead?'

She nodded. 'Okay.'

Their eyes locked. Intense, stomach-flipping, heart-faltering unhappiness, longing and uncertainty bound them together.

Matteo broke his gaze first. He quickly stretched his back in a jerking movement, muttering a curse. 'Stay in Ca' Divina while I'm gone.'

'I can't.'

He shook his head. There was a tense displeasure in the corners of his eyes. 'I need to go back there now, to collect my luggage. My plane is waiting at the airport. Come back with me. You're cold.'

Her throat frozen solid with emotion, she struggled to speak, 'I don't want to say goodbye. Please just walk away.'

For a moment he hesitated. But then he gave a brief nod.

He walked towards her. Her heart fluttered and swooped about her chest. At first she thought he was going to hold her. But his hand touched against hers only briefly before he moved away.

She longed to call out to his retreating back. To halt his long, determined, angry stride.

And then she heard him curse.

He turned around and made straight for her.

He grabbed her.

And kissed her hard.

His mouth, his tongue were demanding. In an instant she was falling against him. Kissing him back just as hard. Needing to feel his strength, his warmth, every single essence of his being.

Her head whirled.

She was losing herself to his taste. To his scent of musk. To the feel of his cashmere wool coat.

She couldn't let go.

And then he was gone.

Pulling himself away. Cursing lowly. Walking away without a backward glance.

But not before she saw the tears in his eyes.

CHAPTER ELEVEN

Wednesday. Four thirty.

MATTEO STOOD AT the entrance to what had been Emma's bedroom. Now it was an empty shell. Just like the rest of the *palazzo*.

He entered the room and walked around it. Restless. Searching. Just as he had searched the rest of the *palazzo*. Searching for some sign of her.

He had hoped that she would have left a note. Some indication of her thoughts before she had walked out.

In the wardrobe he'd found all the clothes he had selected for her. She hadn't even taken the blue hat; he'd found it poking out of the pocket of her navy coat. As if waiting, hoping for her to return.

He propped his head against the carved walnut of the wardrobe door. Weak with weariness and disappointment. She had wanted no reminder of their time together.

Four forty-five.

Across from her bedroom window, on the roof terrace of the house opposite her hotel, an elderly lady tended to her patio garden. She was planting bulbs in flower boxes. Her hands unsteady, she moved slowly but with care. A contented smile on her face.

Had her neighbour ever struggled with a decision? Had she ever been so scared that she felt paralysed with fear?

Emma's fingers stroked the threadbare pelt of Snowy, her toy polar bear, sitting in the palm of her hand. He was staring out of the window too. Looking as bewildered and lost as she felt.

She had rung her best friend Rachel earlier, but hadn't been able to speak to her about Matteo, too upset, her fears too deep inside her to expose them.

What if she went to San Moisè Church and he wasn't there?

What if she went and he *was* there? Waiting. And he said things she didn't want to hear?

Five o'clock.

Emma stopped at one side of the main entrance to San Moisè Church, indecision dancing and colliding with anxiety in her stomach. She steadied herself against a square plinth, the cold stone electrifying her fingertips. The dark green outer double doors were slashed with peeling paint, pushed back to reveal glass-panelled inner doors.

She pulled one of the inner doors open, the fear in her stomach exploding into the rest of her body, leaving her trembling and uncertain if she would have the strength to carry on.

What if he hadn't come? What if he had decided in their time apart that it wasn't love he felt for her after all?

Dusk was settling on the city and the empty church was lit by pale wall lights and hundreds of votive candles, placed in racks and trays in front of bye-altars.

She went and stood by the first pew, her hand touching the grain of the wood. Her heart slowed. She closed her eyes and drank in the calming, distinct and yet light scent of the church: incense, flowers, melting wax.

Centuries of prayer hung in the silent atmosphere. The prayers of the hopeful. The desperate. The fearful.

Her footsteps echoed on the marble aisle. The sound of her aloneness.

She stopped and winced.

Unable to go any further.

Unable to bear the sound of her footsteps.

Knowing he wasn't there to hear them.

She dropped down onto a wooden pew and bent her head.

She had lost him.

What had she done?

And then she heard them.

Other footsteps.

Her head snapped up.

A figure moved behind one of the two thick stone columns that sat before the main altar.

Matteo?

His steps faltered as he approached her where she sat, halfway down the aisle.

Bruised eyes met hers.

His expression was as sombre, as arresting as the knee-length black wool coat, the black cashmere jumper and stark white shirt he wore. He was freshly shaven, and his hair was shorter than it had been before. She wanted to touch him. To feel his smooth skin, hard muscle. She wanted his arms around her. His hands in her hair. The pressure of his body.

Her heart moved beyond her throat to lodge between her ears. Where it pounded to a deafening beat.

His head dropped in a barely discernible nod.

She gave a wan smile in response.

Her bones, her every muscle, her mind all felt weak—powerless onlookers in this event. Her heart had drained every ounce of energy from the rest of her body in a bid to keep working.

She slid along the seat.

Please sit with me. Please let me have a few moments with you.

She didn't look up. Too vulnerable. Too scared he wouldn't sit.

He moved forward, reached her pew. But then stopped.

From the corner of her eye she saw his black trousers, the high polish of his black leather shoes. The neat bows in his laces.

Not moving. Not joining her. A sign of what was to come?

A jolt of pain shuddered through her lungs. A silent wound.

But then he sat. His long legs, muscular thighs grazing against hers.

They swung away from each other at the same time.

He bunched his hands together.

She dared a quick glance.

He was staring towards the altar at an elaborate sculpture showing Moses receiving the Ten Commandments.

She bit down on her bottom lip and closed her eyes. Searing hot pain torched her stomach. She *hated* this distance. This isolation.

And then her breathing slammed to a stop.

His hand was over hers. Holding it. Lifting it up to rest on his leg. His warm, protective, solid hand was holding hers. And not letting go.

Tears filmed her eyes. But she couldn't open them. Not even when the tears ran down her cheeks.

She couldn't stop herself.

His arm went around her shoulder. He drew her in closer. She bent her head and sobbed against his chest.

She couldn't stop herself.

Emma's shuddering body shook against his. He held her closer. Wishing her tremors and tears away.

She had looked at him with distress, sadness, unease as he had walked down the aisle towards her.

Why?

He tugged her closer. Closed his eyes to the slightness of her body. To the jumble of memories that came.

The first time they had made love. The beauty of her porcelain skin in the pale afternoon sunshine. How they had made love later that night in the shower, with a fast and furious need. Urgent, hungry, teeth-nipping lovemaking. As though they were both desperate to leave a mark on the other. Both afraid of how soon they would have to leave one another.

He buried his head into the softness of her thick curls. Inhaled her rose scent.

Her tears stopped. But still he sat there, Emma in his arms. Reluctant to leave the sanctuary of the church.

With slow movements Emma pulled away. She inhaled a deep breath. The breath of emotional exhaustion.

Pink rimmed her eyes, and the tip of her nose was a deeper hue.

She gave an embarrassed smile, her gaze barely touching his. 'I'm sorry—that wasn't supposed to happen.'

'How have you been?'

Her mouth fell downwards before she attempted a smile. 'Honestly? Not great. It's been difficult, these past few days.'

'Me too.'

She blinked hard. Her throat worked even harder. 'I thought you hadn't come...I thought... I thought...'

Her upset slammed into him. Adrenaline and regret mixed nauseatingly in his stomach. He held her hand for a few seconds longer, reluctant to break away, before he stood. They needed to end this agony.

'Let's go and talk.'

* * *

At a small boutique hotel, in a tiny courtyard nearby, he ordered a brandy for them both in the cocktail bar to the rear of the property.

They sat in an alcove, away from the few other customers there.

When their drinks arrived he took a slug of his brandy.

Emma stared at her drink absently before she unzipped and removed her black padded jacket to reveal a cream blouse, with a matching camisole beneath the translucent silk. On her neck hung the fine gold necklace she often wore, scattered with five tiny pendants in the shape of the moon, stars and flowers.

He shuffled in his seat, pushing away the temptation to reach forward and trace a finger along the delicate chain, to feel the pulse at the base of her neck. To be close enough to hear nothing but her breath. To hear her whisper his name. To hear her cries that had wrenched open his heart.

She grasped her glass and drew it in a slow arc across the black lacquered surface of the table. 'Why did you come, Matteo?'

He wanted to turn the question back on her. Have her explain first why *she* came. Still he was uncomfortable at letting his guard down after so many years of building a fortress around his heart.

But he could see the panic, the apprehension,

the fear in her eyes. See how she had paled since they had sat down opposite one another.

Her body was curved towards him. Begging him to speak. To explain.

'I thought asking you to come and work with me would be enough. I told you that I was in love with you. I thought that would be enough. But in our time apart I realised that both of those things would never be enough.'

Her head tilted to the side, as though the weight of her questions was too great.

He answered her by adding, 'I'm guessing that you heard from your ex, from your parents, that they loved you. But that they never proved it.'

Regret tingled at the tips of his fingers and toes.

'There's so much more that I should have told you. I should have found the right words to prove my love. I should have proved it by being courageous enough to say those words. To really open my heart to you. To show you what was deep inside me. But I didn't because I was scared. Scared that by talking I would have to fully face up to just how deeply I love you. And how much it would hurt when you walked away.'

He paused for a moment and looked at her. Tried to garner the energy from her to continue on. A small encouraging nod was all it took.

'All those times the men I'd considered to be a father to me walked away, they took a part of me with them. The innocent, optimistic kid who trusted others was pulled apart bit by bit, until I had nothing left but cynicism and a determination never to be hurt again. I closed down. Refused to love. Refused to ever allow myself to feel that pain again.

'But last night, before my flight, I attended a dinner at a friend's apartment. There was a couple there who reminded me of us. They laughed and chatted together constantly. They were so in tune with one another, so happy. And, watching them, I realised that I wanted what they had. A partner in life. A family of my own. Emma, I want *you*.'

A hand dashed up to cover her mouth, which was dropping open. Her eyes were narrowed with caution and doubt.

'But is it me you want or the *idea* of a partner, a family?'

That was the easiest question he'd ever had to answer. He moved his hands across the smooth table. He opened his palms to her. 'You. Most definitely you.'

She stared down at his hands. And then into his eyes. Still about-to-bolt cautious.

'Why?'

Was this going to work? How had he messed up so spectacularly that she was asking him why he wanted to be with her?

'I wish you didn't have to ask me that question. I wish I'd had the courage to tell you before now. I want you in my life. I love you. I fell in love with you the moment I lay down beside you in my bed. I'm deeply attracted to you, but it's much more than that.'

His heart was throbbing in his chest. Pleading with him—with her—not to let what they had together go. He jerked his hands off the table and curled one fist. He banged it against his throbbing heart. Needing to connect with it. Needing to acknowledge the feelings he had denied for so long.

'It's in *here*—in my heart. A recognition, a familiarity, a sense of belonging together—I don't know what it is, but I know that when I'm with you I'm *me*. There's no pretence. There's no pressure to be something I'm not. I love your elegance, your voice. I love how you mutter in your sleep. I love how you stand with your feet angled, as though you are about to dance at any moment. I love your humour, your touch. I love how you try to act tough when really you're as soft as a marshmallow. You are kind, intuitive...yet strong. I *know* you would fight for those you love.'

He paused. The emotion pouring from his heart was overwhelming his throat. About to drown him in all those words that had been building, building, building in him.

'I love you. I know that might not be enough,

but I can't let you go without telling you all this. You need to know that I will always love you, whatever your decision.'

Emma nodded, and nodded again. As if the forward and back momentum would give her the energy to speak. His words were magical. Beautiful. But she was still scared.

Across from her Matteo, pale, drawn, waited for her to speak.

Deep inside her the truth began to unfurl. She had to open her heart to him. Ask for his support. Trust in him.

But what if he thought she was weak, stupid, needy? What if he didn't like her when she spoke about every deep fear in her heart?

But wasn't that what a true relationship was about?

Hadn't he just been honest with her? And instead of thinking him weak it had made her love him all the more.

On a deep breath she said, 'I came to Venice to heal. To build a wall around myself that nobody would ever penetrate again. I was so tired of being let down. Of my dreams falling apart. And on my first day I met you. Protective, sexy you. A man who didn't want love either. And I immediately fell for you.'

She could not help but smile as a brief, satisfied smile broke on Matteo's mouth.

Then with a shaky exhalation she admitted, 'But it scared the life out of me. I didn't *want* to be in love. So I tried to bury it. Ignore it. But deep within me I knew I was in love from the moment we first kissed. I did everything in my power to tune out the voice telling me that. I told myself that you weren't interested. That *I* wasn't interested. That it was all a rebound fantasy. I looked and looked for a way to find you out, to prove to myself that you would hurt me as much as my ex and parents had.'

She breathed out a guilty sigh. A sigh full of regret.

'When you proposed that I go to Milan and work for you it was the perfect excuse for me to hang on to and justify my fears. Justify walking away when in truth I was in love with you.'

His arm resting on the table, Matteo opened his hand to her, silently asking her to take it. Her fingers curled around his. Her whole body vibrated to a low beat. *Home.*

His voice was low, thick with emotion, when he spoke. 'That's the first time you've said that you love me.'

Was it really? What had she been *thinking*? Had she been so terrified of saying those words out loud?

'I should have told you before but I was scared…scared of dreaming again. I'm petrified something will go wrong. That I'll end up losing you. That something will happen to destroy what we have.'

His fingers tightened on hers, pulled her forward in her seat. He leaned across the table, those brown eyes boring into hers. 'I won't let anything destroy what we have.'

'Do you mean it?'

'Emma, I love you. I want you in my life. Beside me. My mother has spent her life wishing she had done something different. That she hadn't let the love of her life get away. Wondering if he feels the same. Wondering where he is now…what he is doing. If he is happy. I won't live with that regret. I won't let *you* live with that regret.'

'Where do we go from here?'

'I don't want to be without you. Since you came into my life I've realised just how lonely and empty I was before. I'm a happier, better person because of you. I *need* you. I want us to be together. I want us to get married. To be a family. To have children together. Curly-haired, hazel-eyed *bambini*.'

She couldn't help but smile at that image: soft-eyed babies with his golden skin and sucker-punch smiles that would leave her faint with love.

'Are you serious?'

His expression grew stern, as though she had affronted him.

'Do you think I would say those words unless I meant them?'

Her heart skipped a beat at the low, formidable tone of his question, the thin line of his mouth. 'I'm sorry...of course you mean what you say.'

Pain, tenderness, aloneness...all flickered in his eyes.

A bubble of love floated from her heart to her throat, where it popped when she swallowed hard in a bid to concentrate.

Was this really happening?

She had thought they might agree to date, at best.

This was everything she had ever dreamed of. *More* than she had ever dreamed of.

But would she have the courage to say yes?

The courage to believe in such a spectacular, staggering, mind-blowing dream?

To spend her life with the sexiest, kindest, most honourable man alive?

She had come to Venice hoping to harden her heart. But wouldn't doing so—hardening herself, closing herself off to others—mean that her ex, her parents had won? All the people who had hurt her would win?

And *she* would be the loser in all this. She would lose the love of an incredible man. Lose a future full of love. A future of being the mother of Matteo's children.

She would lose the love of her life.

She looked across at him.

He was watching her. Believing in her.

She smiled.

He raised a single eyebrow. Silently asking, *Well...?*

Her smile grew wider. As wide and spectacular as a Dolomites' snow-covered valley. And then she gave a definite nod.

A tentative smile broke on Matteo's mouth, but happiness was carved into the landscape of his face.

He raised his hand and beckoned her to slip along the seat, to sit beside him.

Which she did.

His brown eyes raked over her face, waiting for her to speak.

'I came to Venice to heal, and I did because of *you*. Dancing with you, being held in your arms healed me. Laughing, kissing, making love with you, every tender touch, every eternal gaze healed me. Your compassion, your wisdom healed me. I would be honoured and proud to be your wife. I love you. With you I feel protected, safe, exhilarated. I want to care for you. Love you. I want to spend my life proving to you how much I love you. How deserving you are of love. I promise I will never hurt you. I want to make up for each time your heart was broken as a boy. I want to complete you.'

His hand touched her hair. Then gently he pulled her mouth closer and closer, his eyes packed with love, desire, joy.

In a low whisper, he breathed against her mouth, '*Voglio stare con te per sempre.* I want to be with you for ever.'

Reluctantly, wanting to stare into those magnificent eyes until the end of eternity, Emma closed her eyes. And lost herself to him.

EPILOGUE

THE HOTEL CIPRIANI'S motor boat sliced through the water and Emma giggled and held firmly on to her veil. Rachel, her bridesmaid today, tried to capture it as it flew behind the boat—a fine net sail, catching the attention of the summertime tourists seeking shade from the late-afternoon August sunshine under the awnings of the cafés lining the Grand Canal.

Beads of nervousness exploded in her stomach when the boat slowed to motor up a side canal. They had both wanted to marry in Venice. And what better place than San Moisè Square and Church? The place where they had first kissed. Where they had both found the courage to dream.

With a nervous hand Emma smoothed down the lace skirt of her gown. Tears blinded her vision. What if she hadn't had the courage that day to believe in her love for Matteo? How empty her life would be now.

In the bare six months she had been with him she had gathered a lifetime of memories. Weekends spent here in Venice, in Paris, on Lake Garda, sometimes alone, sometimes with his friends...*her* friends now too. The nights he would arrive in her office, a floor beneath his executive offices, and kiss her neck and earlobes, kiss her into submission so that she would leave early with him—much to the amusement of her new colleagues, who were captivated by the sight of their boss head over heels in love.

What would Matteo think of her dress? Created by the head designer at VMV, the strapless gown had a full voluminous skirt overlaid with fine lace.

At the landing stage, Matteo's grandmother Isabella was waiting for her, shouting instructions to the driver of the boat, who was pretending not to hear her.

Beside Emma, Aurora, her five-year-old flower girl—daughter of Matteo's Marketing Director and her first pupil in the small ballet school she was opening after the summer—hopped up and down with excitement until the driver lifted her with many giggles to deposit her on the landing stage.

When Emma disembarked, Isabella pulled her into a tight embrace, loudly proclaiming, *'Sei bellissima!'* countless times.

Isabella—the woman who had rescued her. The woman who had brought Matteo into her life. She would walk her down the aisle today. Emotion caught in her throat.

Isabella drew her towards the church, her hand at her elbow, saying quietly, '*Lui ti adora*. He adores you, Emma. Thank you for making him truly happy.'

And then Emma was giggling, because a long pink carpet led the way into the church. Not red. But pink. A gift, she suspected, from Matteo. The same ballet-slipper-pink VMV shade as the thousands of roses lining the aisle of the church. The still air sweetened by their heavy scent.

She smiled at the familiar faces beaming back at her from the packed pews. She deliberately sought out Matteo's mum, at the top of the church, knowing how emotional she would be feeling. Knowing that today she was thinking of Matteo's father. They shared a look of understanding, of fondness, of friendship.

And then, inhaling a deep breath, she moved her gaze across the aisle. To Matteo. Who was standing, turned in her direction.

Waiting.

Her steps faltered for a moment.

She felt overwhelmed by how imposing, how handsome he looked in his tuxedo.

He watched her intently. As though this was the most important moment of his life.

When she reached him he didn't move.

For a moment she wondered if he was having second thoughts. But then, his eyes sombre, he leant towards her and whispered, '*Voglio sognare insieme a te per sempre.* Let's dream together for ever.'

She smiled her answer.

And a dazzling smile—a smile that had her heart floating in her chest, that said, *you are the one*—broke on his mouth.

Emma turned to the priest, impatient to become his wife. His best friend. His partner in dreams.

* * * * *

If you enjoyed this book by
Katrina Cudmore, look out for
SWEPT INTO THE RICH MAN'S WORLD
THE BEST MAN'S GUARDED HEART

Or if you'd love to read about another
wedding-themed story, look out for
THE SHEIKH'S CONVENIENT PRINCESS
By Liz Fielding

HARLEQUIN®
Romance

Next month, Harlequin® Romance author

Jennifer Faye

brings you the first book in her Mirraccino Marriages duet:

The Millionaire's Royal Rescue

Tempted by the rebellious royal...

Billionaire Grayson Landers has fled the paparazzi back home—
only to find himself in another media storm: rescuing the
king's niece from a thief!

Lady Annabelle DiSalvo is no pampered princess—she's come
to the Mediterranean island of Mirraccino to solve the mystery
of her mother's death. Grayson can't help but want to help her.
Plagued by guilt over not being able to save his ex, this is his
chance for redemption. Only he absolutely cannot fall for her
and risk his heart again...*unless it's already too late!*

**On sale March 2017,
only from Harlequin® Romance.
Don't miss it!**

Mirraccino Marriages
Royal weddings in the Mediterranean

**And look out for the second book in the
Mirraccino Marriages duet by Jennifer Faye.
On sale June 2017.**

*Available wherever Harlequin® Romance books
and ebooks are sold.*

www.Harlequin.com

HR74425